APOCAL

VOLUME 1:
NIGHTFALL

By Jamie RJ Richmond

WARNING: THIS BOOK CONTAINS SWEARING AND ADULT THEMES AND IS STRICTLY NOT FOR CHILDREN.

For my late mother, Paula,

who taught me right from wrong,

and good from bad.

With thanks to Claire, my dedicated partner,

reader and spell-checker. Without whom,

this book would not be possible.

CHAPTER 1

MR TIBBLES

Jays zipped high in the air above David Sixsmith who was rushing to college. He was already running late again, today it was thanks to a group of local chavs who liked to call him names and insult his family members as he walked past. To them it was banter, to him it was bullying.

As David turned into a council estate to try and get himself back on track to where he needed to be, he noticed the most unusual thing, a woman shouting at a tree. Curiosity slowed his pace and he eventually realised what the real situation was. The old woman's cat was stuck in the treetop, and she was urging it to come back down. David said nothing, but smirked as he attempted to walk past. An attempt that was stopped as the old woman grabbed him with a strength he did not expect.

David didn't ask but she went on to explain that Mr Tibbles often climbs up the very same tree, but is scared of heights so can't get back down, and this event occurs at least weekly. David wanted to run away, he was already late enough, but something made him stay.

"What about the fire brigade?" David asked surprised she hadn't already thought of it.

"They don't like coming. Last time I phoned it took them nine hours to get here. Nine! Mr Tibbles ended up with the sniffles because of them." She complained to David as if she expected him to do something about it. David didn't really want to get into a debate

3

about how busy they were and the fact things like this are probably a strain on the service. So, he simply made a suggestion.

"How about I ring them?" He said, regretting the words as soon as they left his lips.

"Ah, do you not mind pet?" She said grabbing him for a rough hug and a slobbery kiss.

"No not at all." David lied, wishing he had gone down the next street instead.

David pulled out his mobile phone and tapped in the three numbers, he took a deep breath and then pressed call. His little heart was beating as fast as it could, he was terrified. It was finally answered and he went through all the motions. Thirty minutes later and Mr Tibbles was down from the tree, back with its grateful owner. David walked away with a wet cheek feeling like a hero, it was the bravest he had ever been and it felt good. He even pondered going the normal way to college tomorrow. But, he wasn't to know he was about to die.

CHAPTER 2

DEAD AND BURIED

David Sixsmith woke in the pitch black of a coffin ten feet below the cold night soil. He knew it was a coffin because of the shape of his restrictions. He shouted for freedom until his voice was hoarse, but to no avail. Either David was alone, or was being ignored. Both circumstances as equally frightening. It was then that David first noticed the thirst. A thirst that was painful and irritable, not a sensation he was acclaimed to feeling. David tapped around his body for an exit, a clue of how he got there, an item to help him escape. What he was really looking for, was hope. Hope, he wasn't about to die.

A panic overcame him. That's when he began pushing the boards above his head. A dawn of realisation stopped him, he didn't know which way was up. Gravity answered his question as it silently pinned him to his wooden bed. A crash of comprehension snapped him back to his situation. Oxygen. The thought of oxygen brought a sense of panic, a surge of motivation and a hint of breathlessness. David began punching and kicking his way free. In that moment of desperate endeavour, he felt stronger than he had ever felt before. A resilient captive striving for freedom through wood, soil and stone. Twenty-six minutes of desperate flailing and he was exhausted. But he did it, he finally got out. David desperately sucked in oxygen as he watched the soil settle from where he had just escaped from.

He had to wait a couple of minutes for his eyes to adjust to the brightness of the dim lit night, before David realised he was in a cemetery. Dirt ridden and dazed he wandered around the eerie cemetery for signs of life. The croaking of birds and the drift of an occasional car outside the depreciated gate walls, were the only signs of life he could hear. He was soon forced to remember the thirst nagging at his parched throat. He changed his direction towards the water fountain that sprung to mind from his memory of the now familiar environment, Bishopwearmouth cemetery.

He approached the water cautiously as he pondered the cleanliness of the now crooked old steel structure. Too thirsty to care he pressed the button. Water lamely trickled out of the top and after a sigh he began lapping the water like it was the last resource in the world. After a dozen mouthfuls of the murky fluid he realised it wasn't really helping. He used some more to wash himself down and rid the tough grit and loamy soil from his skin.

David looked down into the moonlit water, as it rippled in the metal bowl he struggled to identify himself. As the water settled in the rusty crevice David began to recognise his elements. His hair was black with scruffy looking curls randomly dotted along his head. He moved down to his eyes. A piercing blueness endured from them, it was a startling sight. He was sure they weren't that bright and colourful before. David continued working down his face; everything else looked normal.

Then he noticed his teeth, they were exceptionally white, and they looked huge in the murky water, and fangs protruded from them. He panic-fully felt the area where the fangs were to make sure the murky water was not deceiving him. No, they were definitely fangs. After a few yanks trying to rid them he soon realised that this whole scenario was not some joking scheme or April Fools prank, they were real and they were his.

'*What am I*' he wondered.

CHAPTER 3

LIFE SUCKS

David pondered his next plan of action. He remembered his home and his parents, Mike and Andrea. They were both forty-eight and both unappreciative of him. His father, Mike, was a borderline alcoholic who spent most nights drinking, as well as during the day if he had a reason, and any reason would do. His mother, Andrea, was a hypochondriac who could never be bothered to entertain him. He realised he couldn't go home; especially considering they recently buried him. Besides, they'd probably be disappointed at how terrible he was at being dead.

David searched his mind for an alternative. Only one sprang to mind, Anthony Rydell's house. Anthony, (like David, was a geek and an outcast). He was David's one and only friend. However, his mother was a complete psychopath. The police would no doubt be called if he turned up there. As David pondered a new course of action he scorned his old life. No possessions worth going home for, no memories worth remembering. Nothing to show for himself. He was only eighteen, but it was still depressing.

A raven's croak alerted him back to normality. He had no direction in mind but he knew he had to leave the cemetery; he didn't want to be charged for grave desecration, even if it was his own grave. He took one final look at the epitaph on his now dislodged grave site. It read;

In Loving Memory Of

David Sixsmith

Son of

Mike and Andrea Sixsmith

May 12th 1999 – June 4th 2017

Reading it aloud somehow made it real, enough to produce a single tear which David wiped away before turning his back on his old life. As he eventually neared the freshly painted gates he realised they were locked. Something in him then changed. His walk became a jog, his jog became a run. Before he knew it, David was sprinting as hard as he could. Bitter cold air rushed past his cheeks. He was faster than he used to be, much faster.

Before he knew it, the main gates stood abruptly tall in front of him and it was too late to slow down. With no other option, he jumped. Up and up he went as his eye-line traced him higher and higher. The gates were easy twelve-foot high, impossible to jump. Yet he continued to rise, and was now seemingly going over them. That was until his dangling idle feet caught one of the blunt spikes that perched the very top of the gates. He toppled forward towards the solid concrete road. An instinctive "Ow" yelped from his mouth as he hit the floor, and he hit it hard. For a few seconds, he thought he was done for. He felt numb.

David got up slowly, expecting bodily restrictions to tell him the results of his injuries. There were none. He wiped down the mourning jacket he was buried in and realised there was no blood either. He had got off with a few bumps and bruises after a twelve-foot fall to a concrete floor. One thing was now certain, he was no longer human.

CHAPTER 4

OTHERS

It took David a whole day to realise he needed blood, and he felt much better when he got it. He started off with small insects and reptiles before moving onto rats and birds. He would hide in abandoned buildings by day, and hunt by night. It was the sixth night when he ventured to a nearby woodland to hunt his next meal. A whole manner of animal calls sounded in the darkness, David was accustomed to just a few. He watched the tall trees sway gently in the midnight breeze before he inhaled a deep breath through his nose. Immediately he got the scent of rats and crows and pigeon. He had tried them all. Rats blood the only one worth re-visiting through choice. But he craved something new today. A very something he had now isolated from the array of sniffs now clogging up his nostrils. It moved and David surged after it. It was fast, as was David.

A game of cat and mouse played itself through the forays of the wilderness in fast forward. The difficulty of the hunt excited David so much that a grin emerged through his focused lips. New fragrances drifted among his designated hunts aroma. He tried to rid them as he gained on whatever it was he was chasing. His lungs were almost at full capacity as he noticed the bushy tail of what looked like a rabbit hopping through the underbrush of the woodland. The hunter gained on its prey despite the bracken that continuously blocked his path like deliberate obstacles. He had figured out his bodies limits and could avoid most obstacles with ease. But the fist to his face, he didn't see coming.

Dazed and confused David slowly lifted himself from the leaf scattered earth. A quick glance identified three people in front of him, one pale woman, two pale men. The woman had long wavy ginger hair and was dressed in a white flowing gown, she stood ahead from two men in suits. One of the men was skinny, the other muscular.

"Who are you?" The woman asked.

As an easterly wind blew towards David, he picked up the trio's scent. He wasn't sure what they were, but they weren't human.

"Who are you?" She repeated.

"My name is David. You?" David answered trying his best to sound polite.

"Why are you here?" The bigger of the two men asked while taking a step forward so that he was in line with the woman.

David tried to gulp away the rising fear from his gut as the trio looked at each other as if waiting for a command. David thought the woman was in charge, now he doubted it. It was then that he felt the pain in his cheek. It pulsed through his face reminding him he had been struck.

"What you doing here?" The woman asked clearly frustrated that he had ignored the man's question.

"For that." David's instinctively muttered as he pointed above and behind where the trio stood. As they turned to see what he was pointing at David broke into a sprint in the opposite direction. It was quickly clear there was nothing there. The woman angrily followed him in pursuit. The two men gave each other a glance of reluctance and followed.

As he ducked and dived through the thicket David could smell they were gaining on him, especially the woman. Realising they were faster than him David diverted from his predictable straight line. Problem was, he entered such a randomness he quickly got himself lost and they continued to gain on him. They weren't just faster than him, they were more agile too. David quickly reverted back to a straight line in the hope that the transition would give him advantage enough to escape from the forest.

The trees thinned out and he could finally see the road ahead of him, but David fell to the floor. He had been electrocuted and was unable to move. It didn't make sense. His senses were still working; he could hear and smell the trio as they arrived. David had no choice but to lie face down in the dirt before they picked him up. The only saving grace was that his body was numb. Whatever they were about to do to him he wouldn't be able to feel it.

CHAPTER 5

THE STRANGEST DAY

In the Shropshire village of Ludlow, in a rural area called Stanton Road lived a couple. Helena and Tom Pearce, both 28, were sitting down to a dinner of homemade lasagne and chips. Helena was tall with bleach blonde hair and deep blue eyes. Tom was smart and handsome but desperately needed a shave. He often neglected himself when he simply didn't have the time, and he was always busy lately.

The fact Tom was still wearing his work-wear showed he was more devoted to his job as a salesman, than the job of being a husband. Helena was grateful for the television that quietly buzzed from the front room over the awkward silence they shared in the kitchen. As the telly quietened Helena decided to ask a burning question she had. She was interrupted by Tom's phone; it rang a familiar popular ringtone. Helena previously loved the song, but now she associated it with Tom's busy work-life. He looked at his phone then his wife.

"Sorry love." Tom stated getting up from the chair and swiping the touch-screen of the phone. He walked into the sitting room. Helena listened intently from the other room.

"Yes. Erm...yeah I suppose I could..." he said before looking at his wife around the corner with a forced smile. Helena wasn't too pleased.

"Yeah okay...okay...be about fifteen minutes?... okay...see you then...bye. bye." Tom hung-up the phone and headed towards his wife.

"Work by any chance?" She sarcastically asked.

"Yeah sorry, the cross company didn't get the fax I sent and Steve can't find it on my computer and they can't put through any references 'til that's sorted."

Tom grabbed his duffel coat from the landing and walked back into the kitchen. He shoved another mouthful of lasagne into his mouth, swallowed it whole, kissed Helena on the head, then left.

"Love you...bye." Tom shouted before Helena heard the front door close behind him.

Helena dropped the fork onto the plate, she couldn't stomach any more food when she was this pissed off. After washing the plates down and then steeping them in water Helena walked into the sitting room picking up the Sky remote. The only redeeming feature of Tom being out was that she could catch up on reality TV. As she flicked through the channels trying to remember which channel E! was a figure suddenly appeared in front of her. Helena tried to scream the house down but it was so high pitched she couldn't even hear it herself. Her brain ticked over and she ran to the kitchen for a knife. She grabbed the closest one she could. The shadowed figure laughed as she returned with what looked like a potato peeler. In the time she was absent, the figure had gone from a terrifying shadow to a good looking smartly dressed man. His pink tie somehow told Helena he wasn't a threat.

"Do not panic. I am not here to hurt you, I am here to help." The man stated before rudely removing a framed photo from the windowsill, taking a seat in its place.

Helena was speechless, she had to force out the questions through the panic that was trying to prevent her from speaking.

"Who are you and wha' d'ya want?" She shrieked.

"Like I said... to help." The man replied while looking around the room at the neatly coordinated decoration. "Little too much pine in here, in my opinion love."

"How did you get in here, and help me how?" Helena replied while sneaking towards her mobile phone that sat on the mantel piece above a humming electric fire. The man spotted it, it was obvious what she was doing.

"I'm really starting to get bored of this..." The man disappeared from the sill and reappeared next to the mantel piece. He grabbed the phone before Helena could reach it and disappeared again, he finally re-appeared sitting on the windowsill once more. The mobile was nowhere to be seen. Helena was now angrier than she was scared. She began to march at him with the small knife. His words stopped her dead in her tracks.

"Your husband is having an affair."

Helena didn't know this person at all, but she believed his words. Although she didn't want to.

"What?" Helena asked trying her best not to instantly cry.

"I'm sorry but he's sleeping with his boss." The man replied simply.

"Steve?" Helena scoffed. He was clearly lying.

"Steve is actually Kate, Steve left a little over a month ago. If you ever checked Facebook you'd see he lives in Australia now." The man answered. "Besides it's one of the oldest tricks in the bloody book."

"Wait! How do you know all this, and why are you telling me?" Helena was still in two minds.

"Let's just say I'm helping you now, so you can help me later."

Helena was busy thinking of what to ask next. She had so many questions it was hard to decide which one to go with. She finally picked one but it was too late. The man lunged at her.

She felt his cold hand on hers before the window that stood in front of her disappeared and became a white wall. Helena looked around in astonishment. She had just moved from one place to another, in seconds. She was about to ask their location when it suddenly dawned on her. She was at Tom's place of work. Felted divides split the room into numerous small offices for all of the staff. Stationary and paper littered the desks, large Petra plants and water dispensers coated the edge of the room. A solitary printer stood on a desk.

At the end of the dimly lit room was an office with a light on. It was only then that Helena realised she could hear noises from it. Fresh in her memory was accusations, she marched instinctively towards the office. The fact she had just disappeared from one place and appeared in another no longer fazed her; she headed towards the office for the truth. A few feet away from the door the man who brought her here shouted over to her.

"You could just trust me on this one."

She ignored his words and threw open the door to reveal a couple having intercourse on a desk. The pair recoiled in shock and fell backwards over the table trying to hide their exposed modesty. At first, they giggled, presuming it to be a cleaner again.

"What have I told...." The woman started. She shook Tom to get his attention as she realised who it was. Tom looked at Helena in shock. She responded with a look of disgust. Her grip tightened around the knife she still had in her right hand. Her first instinct was to cut off his balls and slice the woman's throat, but surprisingly her overriding emotion wasn't anger, it was sympathy and relief. She turned her back to the pair and walked back towards the man that had brought her here. Kate and Tom had both spotted the knife and were grateful she hadn't used it. After a pause, Tom went after her, while trying to put his clothes back on.

"Helena, Hel! Fuck!" Tom shouted while struggling with his trousers.

"Get me out of here." A furious Helena demanded of the smartly dressed man that had brought her here. He put down the newspaper he was reading and grabbed her hand.

Tom, now half dressed, was finally catching up to Helena. But then she was gone. Tom looked around gob-smacked and confused. His astonishment conveyed no words. No words at all.

Helena and the man arrived in a darkened street. Only two of the four street lights around them were working. A massive set of metal gates standing tall ahead of them.

"Where am I?" Helena asked. She expected to be took back home, but in a way, she was glad she wasn't.

"Shorebank Wellness Centre for girls." The man answered while adjusting his tie, all this moving around had got it a bit creased. "It's an asylum for the mentally ill."

"Why am I here?" Helena gulped.

"Your sister is here."

"I don't have a sister." Helena's immediate reaction was a shout of frustration and anger. If this was his humour, she didn't like it. But the man's plain expression showed this wasn't a joke. In her mind, she knew he was right. Just like the affair. Once it was said aloud it was real. She had always felt there was something missing in her life. Only now she knew what that hole was.

"Who is she?"

"Margaret Keen, she's in Ward B. Your job is to get her out of here."

"How?" Helena asked, her knees almost buckling. The evening was beginning to get a little too much for her, she began to feel drained.

"Anyway you can." He answered simply.

"How do you know all this stuff, who are you?" Helena turned around determined to get some answers but the man was gone. Helena was alone, scared, furiously angry and downright confused.

CHAPTER 6

THE ROOM

David woke to a blinding white light. A pale headache throbbed through his eyes and imbedded itself as a temporary migraine. It was a welcome reassurance he wasn't dead, yet. With the pain came realisation he was no longer numb, he tried to move but was restricted by something pinning him to what felt like a bed. He gradually opened his eyes to the pasty glare again, half squinting, whilst trying to focus his eyes on something in the room, anything. Computer whizzing and rhythmic beeps played a tune of familiarity in the background. It sounded like a hospital. David panicked for a second.

'What if it was all a dream?' He worried for a moment before appreciating all his recent memories were far too comprehensive to be a dream. The worry though, a realisation, of how desperate he was to be more than human. More than just David Sixsmith.

A dull figure approached causing a welcome shadow in the brightly lit room. David tensed. An inability to move brought an incapability of defending himself. He now knew the true feeling of vulnerability. His eyes gradually accustomed to the room and the shadowy figure became more person than silhouette. Eventually David could make out a face. Big bushy eyebrows moved above green piercing eyes, a broad nose and thin almost blue-tinged lips surrounded by uneven thick stubble. Wrinkles lined his face.

"Finally, we have life." Joked a gruff Scottish accent from above him.

"Where am I?" David asked simply.

"You're in a medical bay. How are you feeling?" The man asked politely.

The man loosened David bonds and let him sit up.

"Ok, I think. Why am I here? Who are you? How'd I get here?"

"Whoa there Paxman, one at a time." The man joked back.

"Sorry I'm a bit dazed... Where am I?" David slowed.

"I'm not surprised kiddo; you were shot with a lightning bullet from a Pulse gun. Basically, you were electrocuted. As for 'where you're at'. You my friend, are inside the medical bay of the Libra Clan's UK Base." The man informed while checking different monitors.

"Thanks..." David added now unsure if this information helped.

"The names Doc by the way."

"David. How'd I get here? Last thing I remember is arriving at a forest."

"Well you're clanless and didn't realise that was a crime, so you're either very dumb, a spy, or a brand-new addition to the vampire meat train." Doc replied before looking at some more of David's vitals.

Doc's attention was shifted to the shouting in the corridor outside, David couldn't quite figure out what the argument was about, only that it was between a man and a woman. It quietened down to silence before he heard footsteps and then a knock at the door.

"Come in." Doc shouted over.

The door opened slowly to reveal a small chubby man that walked with such a limp he needed a walking stick.

"How is he?" The stumpy man asked clearly ignoring David's presence.

"He'll live." Doc answered.

"She's lucky..." the man mumbled under his breath. "Can we give him the serum yet?"

"Yeah I don't see..." The doctor started answering.

"...What serum?" David piped up.

The man raised a little smile clearly happy that David had the bottle to interrupt and ask the question. He walked over to a desk and picked up a bottle of milky-white fluid showing David the contents of the bottle before shaking it.

"This is Lacte Veritas, also known as Truth Serum. And, it'll tell us exactly who you are whether you like it or not."

"How does it work?" David asked.

"You drink, I ask questions, you answer them, simple." The man confirmed before he carefully removed the cork from the little bottle. "You pass, you're free to go. You fail, you'll be permanently detained. You ready?"

"...I guess." David answered hoping to God he didn't fail.

The man shook the bottle before carefully pursing it to David's mouth and pouring it in. David swallowed it. It tasted of soy milk, mixed with metal. David expected an immediate reaction of sorts but as the first question arrived he realised the effects were merely influential.

"My name is Winwood, what is your name?" The man started.

"David... David Sixsmith." David answered with hope that all of the questions would be this easy.

"How long have you been a vampire David?" Winwood asked.

David paused for a second. Having it confirmed to him suddenly made it real. Part of him felt his old life had suddenly disappeared.

"Erm... six days, I think." David eventually answered.

Winwood and Doc looked at the computer monitor with silence. David's palms became sweaty at the thought of his results.

"Who sired you?" Winwood asked looking David in the face.

"I don't know what you mean sorry." David quickly replied with panic in his voice.

His vitals began to jump sporadically. He was worried his ignorance would come across as lies.

"It's okay; just answer as best as you can." Winwood informed attempting to calm David a little.

In the few seconds of silence before the questions continued David thought he heard a creak in the corridor, as if his interview was being eavesdropped.

"Do you know who turned you, who bit you?" Winwood asked next.

"No."

"Have you ever seen or spoke to any other vampires besides us."

"No just you... I think."

Winwood and Doc seemed to tense a little as if their next question would determine his fate.

"Have you ever drank blood?"

"Just animal blood." David was honest, but still he worried whether this was a crime.

"Human blood?"

"No. Never"

"Ok quickly tell us everything you've done since you were sired, turned into one of us." Winwood said before beginning to undo the last of the straps that tied David to the bed.

"I woke up in a coffin, no idea how I got there. I realised I needed blood when I began to hear every living things pulse. I was living on birds and rats blood, when they started drying up I went hunting in that woodland. Then there was three people, they shot me. Next thing I wake up here." David informed as he remembered it, it was as if the potion had re-triggered his memory. Soon he had traced every moment of his journey up to now. After freeing him, Winwood gestured David to follow him out of the room. As they approached the door footsteps sounded away. They were being eavesdropped.

"How did I do?" David asked as they left the room. They emerged into a long corridor filled with blue doors.

"As expected." Winwood answered. "Now I'm sorry about the precautions of a lie detector and the lightning bolt you got from Chora, but with our clan secrecy is integral." Winwood apologised.

"I understand. What do you mean by Clan?" David asked as he slowed his walk to keep in line with Winwood's limp.

"There are different vampire clans, but we will get to that later."

"Now I'd advise you get a bit sleep while the serum wears off, then I will have someone come wake you up and give you a tour of the facility later tonight."

"Thanks." David said as they stopped in front of what looked like a blue cell-door with the number eight bolted onto it.

Winwood gave a simple nod then headed away. David nodded back before heading inside. The room was lit well enough to see everything, but it still had a darkened vibe to it. In the corner of the room was an old looking four-poster bed made up with clean looking sheets and pillows. A state of the art looking television was placed on a set of dark wood drawers. Against the wall sat what looked like a water dispenser filled with a dark red liquid. David didn't need to guess what that was. The room felt modern and antique at the same, he liked it. He decided to have a five-minute lie on the bed and try to take in the last twenty-four hours. Two minutes later he was snoring.

CHAPTER 7

THE TOUR

David woke in a coffin, the air was thin, and he was dying. He struggled with the wood that stood strong above his head, soil spilled through gaps in the boards as he tried to force a way through to no avail. Suddenly, his wooden tomb began shaking as if the cemetery was mid-earthquake. He could hear voices. They called for him to 'wake up'. He quickly opened his eyes to reveal the coffin was part memory, part nightmare.

Now awake, David managed to catch his breath as his eyes adapted to the darkened room; then he finally noticed the figure that had awoken him. It was a vampire he had never seen before. He was dressed in an expensive looking cream suit with a matching shirt unbuttoned half-way down his torso revealing the beginnings of a six-pack. He looked cool and confident. The sunglasses however, seemed inappropriate considering the darkness in the room.

"Sorry I had to wake you; you were having a bad dream." The man apologised. "Are you okay?" He said with a smile.

The apology had a soothing effect on David's racing heart. He realised that if the man had wanted him dead, he would be dead.

"I will be... thanks." David said sitting up on the bed.

"I'm here to give you a tour of the facility, but I will leave you for a minute to catch your breath." The man announced as he headed for the door.

David was keen to see the rest of the facility so he sharply composed himself, washed his face and put on some clean clothes. As he was about to leave the room David's stomach rumbled a loud tune of deep hunger, he knew he would have to drink some blood to rid it. He filled a Styrofoam cup from the dispenser, the gooey red fluid clung to the sides as he swilled it around the cup. He momentarily smirked at the change of his circumstances before proceeding to drink the blood. He drank it quick, like a shot of unattractive alcohol; he winced its fluidity away and headed out of the room like an exuberant teenager on Christmas. As David entered the corridor the man that had awoken him came and introduced himself.

"Hello I'm Trigger." The man said putting his hand out. "I apologise for the circumstances in which our group first met."

"David, and its fine." He replied with a handshake.

Now that it wasn't dark and his heart wasn't racing David could properly take in Trigger's appearance. The man was beautiful, like something ripped straight out of a fashion magazine. The fact he produced two lollies from his pocket and handed one to David just made him seem cooler. David ripped off the packet and read the flavour on the front before putting it in his pocket. 'Bloodberry and Lime'. David put the lolly in his mouth, it was refreshing yet bitter at the same time. It was nice.

As they headed down the hallway even Trigger's walk emanated a swagger. David wished he could be half as cool.

"So, you've only been in your room and the Med-Bay right?" Trigger asked.

"Yeah." David answered keenly.

As they turned the corner the building shot up into the air revealing archways in the ceiling covered in art. Trigger smiled as he watched David's jaw drop.

"It is very easy to forget the beauty in the things you often see."

"Yeah." David agreed with no real comparison in mind.

David was so busy looking at the ceiling he almost walked straight into Trigger as he stopped outside of one of the many rooms in the long corridor.

"This room is our gymnasium." Trigger announced, opening the door for David to have a look inside. It was state of the art gym with every piece of equipment David could think of. It was so impressive David fancied using it, despite never having lifted a single weight in his life. In the room, three people trained. One was a hulk of a man who was busy dead-lifting weights. Another man was using a rowing machine and a red-haired woman was running on one of the four treadmills. David noticed it was the three people from the forest.

"Where's the toilets." He asked quickly heading back out of the room.

"Just over there." Trigger pointed with a confused and embarrassed look on his face.

David disappeared into the loo and emerged a few minutes later looking a little less panicked.

"They're no bother ya know." Trigger announced awkwardly.

"Who?" David asked pretending his sudden disappearing act wasn't about them.

"Them three that scared you off just now." Trigger said with a smile and a pat on the back.

"They didn't." David lied.

There was an awkward silence as Trigger figured out the best way to say what he was thinking. They slowly walked the corridor while he pondered.

"You don't have to pretend with me, I understand. I was the same when I first come here, I was a bit of a coward to be honest, that's why Winwood put me on weapons and logistics, so I had no choice but to face my fears."

David didn't know what to say, so he said nothing at all.

"They were just doing their job. This place is supposed to be a secret, yet there's always vamps and other creatures turning up in the forest unaware of our location underneath it."

"We are underneath the forest?" David shouted, giddy with excitement.

"Yeah cool right. Yeah, we are sort of the police of the vampire world and we must keep everything a secret. Plus, everything's a bit tetchy because Chora got a bit of a strange palm reading a few weeks back." Trigger informed.

David felt more at ease now, more relaxed, more confident.

"What was the reading?"

"Most of it was the same confusing psycho-babble you usually get with palm readers. You will meet someone new, you will fall in love blah blah blah. But this woman said *some of your friends will die in the storm. A storm the like of which, we have never seen before and will never see again*'. I have told her it's probably crap but she believes in that type of stuff..." Trigger reasoned.

"...That's why they shot you with a Pulse gun." Trigger added.

For some reason, it brought a smile to David's face. Like he didn't mind being shot anymore, they had a genuine reason for it. As Trigger showed David a bunch of non-descript rooms such as meeting rooms and other bedrooms David's confidence grew and grew.

"So, who were them people in the gym, the people I met in the forest." David asked as Trigger showed him around a kitchen and then a dining room and then a store cupboard. There was boxes and boxes of stuff, it looked like a hoarder's paradise.

The big one's Torus, he's sort of our personal trainer, slash martial arts teacher. The other bloke was Legitus. He is our main investigator and representative, he knows the law like the back of his hand. The woman is Chora, she deals with all the stocks and supplies and she's also second-in-command behind Winwood, who you met earlier this morning.

Trigger next showed David what looked like a sports hall full of red mats, it was no doubt used for martial arts and fighting practice. Placed on the walls were an array of weapons which looked like they had been blunted. As the pair walked back into the neoclassical corridor David was intrigued what room was next, but he began to wonder whether his stay was permanent or not.

"What will happen to me after this tour?"

"I think Winwood intends you to stay the night. Tomorrow he's taking you to London to pick a clan." Trigger announced. David's look of puzzlement told Trigger he needed more information.

"We are Libra clan, one of twelve groups to choose from, every vamp must have a clan, each clan is different."

David thought for a moment.

"Who do you think I should pick?" David asked excitedly.

"Whoever feels right for you I suppose?" Trigger replied.

The pair walked to the end of the corridor. It was apparent the tour was coming to an end.

"The door to the left is the washroom area. Its complete with showers, toilets, bathtubs etc. Pretty ordinary really. But this..." Trigger said opening the door to the right. "...is by far the coolest room we have in this place." David followed him in.

He walked into a face full of amazement. Wall to wall shelves, shelf to shelf of books. The middle of the room contained an island filled with desktop computers. David was in his element. He ran over and scanned through the A-Z directory of books looking for his idols. All of his favourite books were there, even the rare ones, and most were first editions. David rarely ever swore but this time he couldn't help himself.

"This... is... fucking... awesome."

"Isn't it!" Trigger beamed as David spanned the shelves like a child in a sweet shop.

"Now, I can't leave you unsupervised and I have to go out. But please, feel free to borrow one to take back to your room." Trigger informed upon seeing how late it was. The tour had taken twice as long as he expected it to. David quickly scanned the shelves some more. He noticed the works of Shakespeare, Rowling, Lewis, Tolkien and Martin but he had read all their stuff. He wanted something new. A smile lit up his face as he finally found the perfect book.

'Vampires. A complete History.' by Garfield Cassidy.

The pair headed back without a word as David silently contained his excitement. He was looking forward to reading his book and he was looking forward to tomorrows trip. He had never been as far as York, never mind London. He was also looking forward to picking a clan, even though he wasn't quite sure which one he was going to go for.

"Good luck, and all the best for the future." Trigger said as they arrived at the door to David's room.

"You too." David said, and with a little handshake they parted ways.

David had a quick drink of blood, got comfy on his bed and read until he fell asleep.

CHAPTER 8

INSANE ASYLUM

Helena had stood in front of the big metal gates for nearly two whole hours. She had no idea how she got there, well she did, she just wasn't sure if she believed it yet or not. Her whole life had been turned upside down in a matter of hours. A cold drip of rain splashed lamely against her forehead bringing her out from her daydreaming state. She had been reliving the night over and over in her mind since some man had transported her here and told her she had a sister inside. She was trying her best not to think about the cheating of her husband and all the hurt that come alongside it.

As the cold rain began to dance around her feet Helena tried to push the gates forward. They stood firm and locked. She looked around for a bell or a knocker. A small grey electronic box with a green button caught her attention. She pressed it for a few seconds, no reply. Helena looked up through gaps in the gates. She could make out part of a driveway that led to an old-looking building stood firmly on top of a hill. There were no signs of life in there.

"This is ridiculous." She said aloud as the cold of the rain began to give her the chills.

She pressed the button once more and waited.

She was about to turn away when one single light flickered on in the west wing of the building. It was a small looking room on the ground floor, the type a security guard might use. She saw a door swing open and a hooded figure leave. It began walking down the road towards her. It was obvious it was an elderly person as it took him so long to get down by the gates. She could make out the face of an old man as he approached her. He had big bushy eyebrows on top of a pair of angry wide eyes, they were unusually green. Underneath were wrinkles that seemed to span the rest of his face. Towards the bottom of his face lay cracked lips above a chin full of cuts from a previous shave. The man stared at Helena through his beady eyes before pulling his blue waterproof coat-hood forward to block out more of the rain.

"Hi there. I was wondering if you have a place for the night?" Helena asked using the first thing that came to her mind. She regretted the words the instance they left her lips.

She was answered with a sudden bright light in the face as the security guard shone a torch into her eyes to take a closer look. Helena scuttled back a yard out of its brightness.

"This isn't some random hotel if your drunk ya know." The old man stated.

"Erm...Yeah. I know that."

Helena was struggling for words and she felt ridiculous. Then it suddenly occurred to her, to get into a mental institute all she had to do was pretend to be mental, and what was more mental than the night she was having. She decided she would offer the truth to see what happens.

"I was at home, then a man appeared from nowhere and took me to see my husband who is having an affair, but then he brought me here and told me I have a sister."

She rushed her words but felt good to be rid of them, she felt like she had control of her life again. The old man looked mystified, but nonetheless he shuffled through a set of keys and began opening the gates. When he finally managed to open the gates and let Helena in, she didn't know what to do or say next.

"Follow me." The old man said after making sure the gate was locked, several times.

Helena entered the compound and gazed at the huge building that lay ahead of her on top of the hill. It was beautiful, yet creepy. Half eroded gargoyles perched the roof. All of the windows were dressed with plain white sheets and big black bars. They were there to keep people in, not out. The walls were thick with a pebble-dashed stone coating over the brick foundation. You could tell from where the coating had eroded away.

Helena was surprised to see the old man walk straight past the building and up towards a single two-level building placed beside it. As they arrived Helena made out a sign on the wall.

"MR. JEWSON – HOSPITAL MANAGER"

The old man knocked on the front door with a few loud bangs. It seemed to take several minutes to be answered and during this time the man didn't utter a single word to Helena. The man that eventually answered the door was a sight for sore eyes. He was an extremely overweight man in his fifties with a large bald head who had answered the door in his curry-stained dressing gown. He adjusted his glasses to see who it was. Helena could see bags under his eyes.

"What is it now Alf, are you aware how late it is, and... who... is... this?" The man asked tilting his head with mystery like a shaved pug.

Helena could feel the warmth exuding from the house. She began to shiver from the cold she was in.

"Sorry to bother you sir but this one was standing at the gates, told me somebody transported her here." The security guard informed very slowly, he exaggerated what he felt was the important words in the sentence.

"Ah thanks Alf, you better come in then m'lady." The bald man stated opening the doorway wider. Helena expected him to move and let her in, he didn't. She had to squeeze by him to get inside. She could feel and smell his sweat as she did so. But the warm blast of the house was too tempting for Helena to refuse.

"Thanks Alf bye." The bald man finalised, closing the door behind Helena.

As she began to warm through, her ears picked up the sound of classical music playing quietly from another room. Her nose plucked up at the smell of enticing scented candles. She recognised the smell to be lavender. Her skin could feel the warmth of a fire burning from a nearby sitting room. The man adjusted himself to look presentable in just his dressing gown. He stuck his sweaty palm out, Helena pretended she didn't notice it as if she was too busy looking around.

"I'm Mister Jewson, but you can call me Terry. I bet a nice drink would warm you up a little. But for now, why don't you go and grab a seat by the fire." He insisted before fleeing into another room. Helena walked into the sitting room without a word. She was shocked by the beauty of the room. It had immaculate woven carpets sitting in front of a black marble fire-place. Wood logs cracked within the fire, the flames dancing around them. On the walls lay elegant mirrors, and antique guns. It reminded Helena of a posh hotel lodge she had stayed in many years ago.

"Is brandy okay for you? I'm afraid I am out of tea and coffee?" Came a booming voice from the other room.

"Yeah." Helena answered trying to take in the rest of the room before she sat down next to the warm fire.

She began looking at a stuffed deer head that lay opposite her on the wall when Mr Jewson re-entered carrying two glasses similar to chandelier crystals, both half-filled with a thick brown liquid.

"Extremely sorry about my appearance dearie. I get night terrors and sweat a lot." He stated handing her one of the glasses before taking a seat opposite her.

"It's okay." She answered taking a tiny sip of the so-called Brandy. It tasted vile but warmed her throat which was pleasing.

"Also, I don't normally get visitors at this late an hour. Go on drink more... It will warm you through, you look freezing."

"I am pretty cold." Helena agreed as she brought the glass back up to her mouth.

She took a larger gulp. This time it didn't just warm her throat but her whole mouth.

"Very good, very good." He said putting his glass down and standing up.

Helena then thought she felt her whole face warming up, then her shoulders. Then she realised it wasn't warmth at all, it was numbness, and it was spreading like wildfire. She had to get away.

She turned on heel to head for the door as Mr Jewson headed towards her. But it was too late and she fell to the floor in a lump.

CHAPTER 9

MYSTERY JOURNEY

It was the next morning and David and Winwood slowly walked along the luminous modern corridor towards a blank wall. Winwood's limp prominent as they walked in tandem.

"How was your tour?" Winwood asked as an icebreaker.

"It was awesome." David quickly answered clearly concentrating more on the blank wall ahead of him, than on the question.

"I suppose you are wondering where we are going." Winwood asked, he could tell David was distracted.

"London." David simply answered.

As the pair arrived at a seemingly blank wall at the end of the corridor they stopped. Then Winwood did the most unexpected thing. So, unexpected in fact that David temporarily questioned his own sanity. He watched bewildered as Winwood waved at the wall as if it were a friend he had known for years. Attempted thoughts of explanation pulsed through David's mind. Was this a test, an illusion? Was he the butt of a joke? Perhaps he was still underground in a coffin wallowing in his own waste and had hallucinated everything since, including this.

But suddenly, as if answering his question and confirming his own and Winwood's sanity, an oblong shape seemed to be revealing itself from within the wall. It revealed a small room, apparently pointless room. Yet David stood there in amazement, his eyes transfixed wide open. Thousands of words made up his David's personal vocabulary, his very own distinctive dictionary of communication and all he could manage for this situation was a single word.

"Mint!"

David hadn't seen anything like this in his life; it was like magick, but real magick. He watched as Winwood walked in and turned to face him. David inspected the room as he followed Winwood inside. It had no visible exit, other than the one they had just used as an entrance, no windows lit the room, nothing of note stood above, or below them. It was anti-climax incarnate. Then, suddenly the room began to move.

"It's a lift." Winwood announced taking a firm hold of the handrail that lined the room. "I suggest you hold on." He finalised with a smile. With that the lift went shooting up into the air. David desperately fumbled for the bar as his feet began rising from the floor from the sheer speed of the lift. He white-knuckled the lift ride to its halt before finally breathing out. His lungs exhumed the panic that he had swiftly sucked in. Ahead of him a set of doors opened to reveal a darkened forested area. Before that David needed a full minute to regulate his breathing. As he began to settle he pondered the use of oxygen as a vampire and intrigue forced a question.

"Do we need oxygen?" He asked as they began walking through the forest.

"Of course, we do. Why wouldn't we?" Winwood replied with a laugh. "Come on. This way."

Alerted back to his surroundings David immediately recognised the forest. He wasn't far from where he was shot with something the Doc called a lightning bullet. As he walked away from the base he began to realise how much he wanted to stay. It wasn't long until the thick bracken and branches thinned out and they found themselves heading into a shady roadside car park complete with a wooden fenced border. Parked haphazardly in the far corner was a black car with tinted windows. It was almost presidential aside for the dints, rust and mud splats that became apparent upon closer inspection. The headlights shone straight ahead into the murky air to reveal a host of buzzing insects. Winwood approached the car expectantly as he opened the back door for David. The interior was surprisingly roomy and elegant. Leather seats, cup holders and array of buttons told David this was once the pinnacle of luxury road travel.

"David. Ryan...Ryan. David" Winwood input an introduction.

Ryan, the driver, squeezed a gloved hand through a hole for David to shake. His black chauffeur hat was equally dark as his skin, his grip was strong, for a human. David realised he could smell him, a tone of fragranced meat wafted through his nostrils like seasoned pork. His vampiric instinct drove his eyes straight to the man's wrist. David began to hear Ryan's blood pulsing through his body, and he wanted it.

"Well. What do you think?" Winwood asked deliberately distracting David from his instincts.

"What sorry?" David asked.

"What do you think of the car." Winwood reiterated.

"Yeah it's nice. Is it yours?" David asked, relieved as the car pulled away.

"It belongs to the clan." Winwood answered half-proud.

It wasn't exactly a crib of exquisite vehicles, but it was something David thought.

"Cool." David put forward. He felt guilty for his temporary lust. He wanted to talk about it but then decided he had a more pressing question to ask. "How does this clan thing work then?"

"Every vampire has many choices to make. One of them is which clan to join. That's where we are going now, to get you a clan."

"Why do I have to pick a clan, can I not just join yours?"

Winwood received David's words as a compliment. It forced a smile through his wrinkled face. He suited it.

"I'd love that, but unfortunately it's not the way we do things anymore. You have to do what is called the trial of clans."

"What's that?" David asked with genuine intrigue.

"A representative of each clan puts forward their case to have you. You simply choose which clan you want to join."

"How many are there and how do I know which one to pick?"

"There are twelve clans. You will ask a series of questions and every clan will give you an answer to each question. After every clan has answered your question, you must evict one. It's simple enough. As for who to pick I cannot answer that. I would simply advise you, to go with your gut." Winwood informed.

"Is there much difference between the twelve clans?"

"Honestly. Yes. But that's for you to find out with your questions when you get there. For now, I would get some sleep if I was you, we have a long journey ahead."

"Ok." David finalised.

He didn't think he would be able to get much sleep and decided to just lie with his eyes closed for a time. He began to think of his Mam, his Dad and best friend Anthony. His memory etched their faces clearly in the forefront of his memory. He would have loved to have shared this experience with Anthony. As his memory of his best-friend flashed in tandem with the successive swath of street-lamps David began to doze off. David dreamed while he slept. For a while he was back playing computer games with Anthony every night. There was nothing better in the world than clocking computer games together with a pizza meal and a few cans of pop. Suddenly, a voice seemed to be coming through the computer calling his name.

"David. David." The vibration of the control pad got stronger. Then he woke to the sound of Winwood's voice back inside the fancy old limousine. David temporarily scorned his old life as he followed Winwood through busy streets of people. Eventually he found himself on a train.

"DAVID! DAVID! Quick, strap yourself in." Winwood shouted as a buzzer began sounding. David snapped back to reality and instinctually strapped himself to the nearest wall with a strap similar to a seatbelt. He realised there were no seats on the train, just straps attached to the walls and floor. The train started normally and David questioned the use of the strange seat belts on the train. The reason became apparent as his view of outside the train dissolved into a blur as the train quickly picked up speed. David was scared to move, then he realised he couldn't anyway. The speed of the train pinned him to the wall. His insides felt like they were moving, like hundreds of butterflies playing a game of hide and seek in his stomach. He didn't like it.

"How long?" David shouted through gritted teeth as the train reached its maximum speed.

"An hour." Winwood shouted back through fits of laughter. It was the first time he had laughed in months.

CHAPTER 10

BFF

It was 7 A.M and Anthony Rydell awoke to shouting. It was his mother trying to get him up for college. He groaned and shouted back down.

"I'm up, I'm up."

Anthony swivelled to sit on the edge of the bed. He pondered for a moment and realised he was beginning to get sick of living with her. She constantly nagged at him and was really strict about him going out. He knew deep down she was just overprotective because his father was killed by a car when he was little. But still, she was smothering him.

Then he remembered. Remembered the loss. That feeling of being smacked in the gut as he thought of his friend David. He quickly thought of something else to temporarily rid the hurt that made it hard to breathe. A distraction from the torturous emotion pulling on his heartstrings. Escapism from reality. Deep down he knew, he knew when he let himself go back there it would hurt even more. but he wasn't ready to face it yet. He couldn't accept David was gone.

He distracted himself by getting ready. He threw on clean underwear and socks partnered with the t-shirt, tracksuit bottoms and hoodie he had worn the day before. Once ready, he sluggishly headed down the carpeted stairs. His mother Wendy was waiting for him in the kitchen. Her bright blonde hair and bright red lipstick meant you could easily pick her out in a crowd. Light blue eye shadow caked her eyes and she seemed full of joy. She was busy cooking Anthony breakfast in her favourite apron; it was full of different types of cakes. Anthony could smell the bacon and toast the instant he entered the room.

"Finally, you're up." She said before getting the toast out of the toaster.

Anthony managed to utter nothing more than a groan of acknowledgment.

"You are getting up later and later each morning. One would think you are losing interest in college. You aren't wearing that again are you?" Wendy stated as she handed him his breakfast of fried eggs, two heavily buttered slices of toast, bacon, sausage and mushrooms. Anthony tried to force a smile of thanks. He wasn't feeling very hungry if he was honest. He grabbed a fork and began eating the eggs anyway.

"I've told you, you don't have to do me breakfast every single morning mam." Anthony reminded her before forcing some more egg into his mouth.

"Breakfast is the most important meal of the day." She insisted while tidying up.

The conversation was a weekly song that always ended on the same note.

"Mum, I want to talk." Anthony suddenly announced pushing his plate away.

His mother's mood suddenly changed to worry. Worry about what he was going to ask or say. She stopped tidying and sat down.

"I've been thinking, and..." He paused as if scared to finish the sentence. But then he come out with it anyway.

"...I'm not going to college today... or the rest of this week in fact." Anthony sternly stated. He gulped down his fear of her reaction and tried to keep a confident look on his face.

"Why ever not honey, are you being bullied, are you struggling with the coursework, is it a girl?" Wendy quizzed back. Her upward infliction on the final sentence told Anthony she was more worried about a girl than him potentially being bullied.

"No." Anthony firmly answered. "I just need a break." He said with a deep breath.

"But there's only a few months left and then you're finished for six weeks and then we can go on holiday to Algarve to see your Auntie June. That will be a good break for you." Wendy countered.

"For God's sake NO!" Anthony replied with a raised voice. It was the first time he had ever raised his voice to her, but she wasn't listening and he needed her to. He wasn't backing down this time. His mother looked startled by his reaction.

"I need time to breath, time to think, time to... grieve." Anthony released. He could feel a tear forming in the bottom of his right eye. But the tension in his body seemed to suddenly dissipate. He had been building everything up since his friend was killed. There was a long pause of mutual respect.

"You're absolutely right son." His mother agreed getting up from the table. She headed over to a bottom draw, opened it and pulled out a packet of cigarettes stored underneath cookbooks. She opened the half empty packet taking one out and lighting it with a green lighter from the box. She closed her eyes and took one long drag. Her smoking was a revelation to Anthony, he didn't know what to say. He was glad when she started to speak.

"Since your Dad, I've been so on top of you, you haven't had a second to realise who you are, or what you want. You don't have to go to college or on holiday with us for that matter." His mother sympathised.

"The holiday is fine mum, even though it's with your mad sister." Anthony said truthfully.

They both laughed and the tension dissolved.

"... and college is fine, I just... need to do something else first. I need to know what happened to David."

Anthony tried his best not to cry as he got up. His mother's eyes filled with tears.

"I know son. If you need anything though, you just let me know yeah?"

"I will. Thanks."

Anthony got up with a new confidence. He kissed his mother on the cheek before getting a slice of toast. As he went to leave his mother crumpled a twenty pound note into his hand.

"Just don't do anything stupid and please remember to eat something, yeah?" She ordered with a smile.

"I'll be fine mum, don't worry." Anthony finalised before leaving the house.

Anthony walked. He had no idea which direction he was going, or location he was heading to. He staggered around aimlessly while contemplating things in his head. Then a sudden thought stopped him dead in his tracks. The newspaper said he had been murdered with poison and that was the cause of death. However, in most of the TV crime shows Anthony had seen (and that was a lot!) toxicology reports usually took six to eight weeks. David was buried within a week. To Anthony that could only mean two things. Either they hadn't done a proper autopsy or David's body wasn't in the coffin when it was buried.

CHAPTER 11

HEAD OF HOUSES - PART ONE

After a little under an hour strapped to a wall and put through extreme G-force David was so relieved to see Winwood un-strapping himself as the train came to its second and final stop. (He had hoped the first stop around half way through was it!). As they exited the train carriage David struggled to maintain his balance, the journey had obviously disorientated him.

"Thanks for the warning." David joked as they headed up an escalator.

"If I'd have warned you, would you have come on the train?" Winwood asked.

David thought for a second before answering.

"Probably not if I was given the choice, no."

"That's why I didn't warn you. Besides it was fun was it not?" Winwood asked with a smile.

"If you call feeling your organs moving around your body fun... than yeah." David sulkily replied still trying to catch his breath and stabilise himself. "Just please tell me we aren't going back the same way."

"After today I might not ever see you again. You may not be leaving with me remember." Winwood reminded him.

"Oh yeah." David replied with a rising tide of nervousness. That thought had not even occurred to him until then.

The pair walked in silence through a bunch of train station corridors until they arrived in a giant circular green room with an old oak desk dominating it. Sat there was a man dressed in a judge's formal clothes, he sat reading a stack of papers. David could tell he was a vampire from the smell. Vampires somehow smelled of old and new at the same time, like fresh dust. As the pair approached the desk, the man spoke.

"Oh, your here." The judge announced not looking up from the papers. "You can go up now Winwood. I'm sure the boy will be fine with me for a minute or two."

David was confused how the judge had deducted such an accurate assessment without even looking up.

"You'll be alright?" Winwood asked David.

"Yeah I think so." David hoped.

"Well good look kid, it was nice to meet you and I wish you well in whatever you choose." Winwood extended out his hand. David shook it with a "Thanks."

After Winwood left the room David stood bored for what seemed like twenty minutes before the judge stood up grabbing a wooden gavel from the desk and heading towards a big metal door. David was starting to hate doors and more importantly what stood behind them. He wasn't surprised to see a small room with metal bars lining the room, it was clearly another lift. He held on and closed his eyes.

The lift quickly reached the basement and a set of orange and brown decorated doors opened ahead of them. From outside the room all that was visible was a solitary green stool. As David and the judge walked towards the room, their footsteps echoed aloft. Each step unable to silence the previous. As they entered, the room stretched out to show numerous rows of seats. It spanned around them like an oval theatre. If the seats were the audience David was about to be centre stage as he was gestured to sit in the green stool that stood idle and central. As he attempted to get comfortable he began to pick up other little details about the room. Scratches on the hard-wooden floor indicated either the chair often moved around or other chairs had been present at some point. Metal loops attached to the floor indicated some people were brought here against their will, probably for criminal trials.

David then noticed the chairs. Two rows of six elegantly carved redwood seats stood apart from the other seats in the room. Each with a different logo woven into the back-supporting pillow. The house name exquisitely engraved above. Middle of the top row was the only name he recognised, Libra.

"Are you ready?" The judge asked from a desk behind David, giving him a shock. David had completely forgotten he was there.

"Yeah." David replied unsure of what exactly what was about to happen.

"Just relax, it's all relatively straightforward. My advice to you is to choose your questions and eliminations carefully. This is a decision not to be taken lightly as you're stuck with that choice for a minimum of fifty years from today." The judge declared.

Truth be told the judges' advice had made him feel even more anxious. He was forced to swallow the rising nervousness as the judge banged his gavel to start proceedings. The people that entered were the strangest collection of people David had ever seen in his life. One familiar figure stole David's attention, Winwood. Once all twelve were seated the judge banged his gavel once more.

"Today's first trial is for a new-sire called David, we are unaware of his sire. Libra found him just yesterday, no human contact and no sires of his own. No abilities registered yet. Are all clan's present and ready?" The judge bellowed across the room, his voiced echoed repetition through the great hall before echoes of agreement silenced them.

"We all know how this goes, so let us begin with our first question please David." The judge declared.

Silence filled the room as David desperately searched his mind for a question. Nothing came. Several questions had sauntered through his mind before he came in. Half he had now forgotten, the other half upon reflection, seemed like silly questions. David was happy to shut up the silence when his first question finally came.

"What would I be doing in your clan?" David relayed across the room. Now that he'd asked it, it seemed the most obvious question in the world to ask. The man representing Hierophant was dressed in a lovely purple encrusted saree; he stood up first and answered, his voice was kind and Asian accented.

"You will be learning about vampire history, inner strength and how to teach others the same." He declared before sitting back down.

David loved learning, and thought they had good morals. They were an early option at least.

The Dionysus clan member stood next. She was dressed in rags, had face tattoos, umpteen piercings and topped off her look with a red-dyed Mohawk. She practically screamed her answer.

"The only thing you'll learn with us is how to party." She answered with a grin.

Her answer brought a laugh to proceedings and David relaxed. The Rat clan member stood up next and answered. He was dressed in a laboratory-technician's outfit and had clearly come straight from work. He looked meekly and carried a nervous disposition. David detected fear in his voice.

"We want to improve all vampire life through science and technology and you will be an integral part of our research team."

The Loki clan member stood next. They were represented by a ridiculously tall and thin woman wearing a leopard print top; she looked like she could be related to a giraffe, but she spoke more like a mouse.

"You will be given money to start your own business." She practically whispered.

Gaia countered next. David thought their representative looked so short and stumpy that he could be related to a cannon ball. His voice was deep and nasal, like that of a manly man, but one with a cold.

"Most of your time will be spent praying and finding ways in which to help others."

David was surprised at how different, yet individually brilliant each clan sounded. This was going to be a harder process than he originally thought. Next to stand and answer was Winwood. He was obviously representing Libra.

"With us you will learn to solve crimes, situations and arguments." With that Winwood sat back down.

Two words sprung to David's mind *'Vampire Cop'*. In his head that was the coolest two words he could put together. Part of him had already decided to pick Libra, but the fifty-year escape clause had at least presented an air of caution. He had to have an open mind.

CHAPTER 12

HEAD OF HOUSES - PART TWO

David remembered the job at hand and concentrated on the ongoing proceedings. The next representative was for a house named Lascaux. She looked like a crazy old homeless woman.

"With us you will help us create new ideas for an art or building project."

The Tiyu man looked carved, muscles protruding through his thin t-shirt. He answered

"The next vampire sports tournament is just sixteen months away. You will be training for this."

Trinity was next. There for them, was a hippie looking man with a beard. He responded.

"We will be like…totally involved in bringing together like… not only other clan's, but like… other races of people and things."

His voice was slow and exaggerated like he was drunk or stoned.

Representing Solus was the most ordinary looking woman David had seen in the vampire world, she almost looked human. She spoke more fluently and clearly than others.

"Vampire segregation from the human population far precedes the standing of other clan's priorities. You will help us achieve that said objective."

Jinn's rep was an overweight man dressed in long orange robes. He spoke with a strange raspy-ness to his voice like an avid smoker.

"You will be helping us find our creator, the Jinn." He answered before taking a deep breath and sitting down. He sounded like he had just run a mile. The other clan representatives gave the vampire a funny look. Only Winwood and two others seemed unfazed by the man's answer.

Last to answer was a woman, who looked more like a man. She represented Unus and she spoke like she was at a rally, not a hearing.

"You will help us find a reasonable way to get rid of the snakes and rats of the world like werewolves and ghosts."

'Werewolves and ghosts are real.' David thought to himself. For a moment he didn't register what was going on around him. He was in shock.

Silence followed for a minute before the judge spoke again.

"You have heard every response to your first question. Please eliminate one of the clans from selection."

David didn't even have to think about it. He did not like the sound of the last person's answer. He looked up at the clan name.

"I would like to eliminate Unus please." David spoke clearly but politely.

The male-looking female representative stood up looking rather cross, before storming out of the room. David felt kind of bad for her, but he definitely didn't want to join that clan.

Over the next hour, David began to eliminate more of the clans as they answered each of his questions. After Unus was Gaia. They sounded boring and spent most of their time praying. After that he eliminated the House of Solus because he didn't want to live underground never seeing other creatures. Jinn was next to go because they seemed to be obsessed with finding genies. The next two houses to be eliminated were Tiyu and Lascaux, this was because David felt he wasn't the right person to help with sport or art. He appreciated both, but wasn't very good at either.

The next house to leave the process was Dionysus; all they seemingly wanted to do was party. He thought that notion would get repetitive after a while. The House of Trinity was gone next; he liked the idea of their values but didn't fully understand exactly what he would be doing. Next to go was Rat, David loved the idea of science and technology but was really struggling to find faults in each of the houses now. But by this time the lab technician representing this house seemed to be disinterested in being there.

Only three houses remained, Loki, Hierophant and Libra. Libra, represented by Winwood, had an amazing facility, he knew the people and he was interested in what they do. The woman that shot him with a Pulse gun was the only fault he could think of. With Loki, he would get to start his own business. David revelled in the thought of being his own boss and ideas were already running through his head. Their rep was the giraffe looking woman. Her downside was that some of her words were too quiet to hear, and some sentences sounded too good to be true, almost scripted.

Lastly was Hierophant who seemed obsessed with learning. It reminded David of his former life and he craved some normality in all this newness, and their rep was the man in the saree who seemed so nice. But David felt he needed an aim or an objective to work towards, Hierophant just didn't seem to have one. His thoughts were interrupted by the judge.

"Only two questions remain. Choose them carefully."

Just then, David thought of a brilliant question, it seemed to come from nowhere.

"Excluding your own house. If you were in my situation which house would you choose?" David asked rather pleased with himself. He looked up at Winwood who was grinning at his clever question.

The Hierophant representative stood and looked at his two options. "Libra." He simply said before sitting. Winwood was next to stand. "Hierophant." Next to stand was the woman from Loki who looked cross and almost lost for words.

"Libra." She disapprovingly muttered before sitting down.

"So, your next eviction is...?" The judge asserted.

"Loki please." David announced.

The tall woman from the Loki clan sulked away while David pondered his final question.

He had to think for a good five minutes before a question came to mind. He felt he knew everything he needed to know about each house already. He was cautious with his words.

"What makes the other clan better than your own?" David asked.

The genius of the question was beyond his comprehension. David had surprised everyone, even himself. For a while there were no words to be had, Winwood was first to find some.

"I think...Whether you are a vampire, werewolf or human this world is a horrible place to live in. Hierophant is a great house striving to change that. Libra tries to contain the bad and to keep it from harming the little good that's left in this world. Whereas Hierophant truly does see the good in all people and encourages it. Only a fool would pick a life of danger over such a wonderful moral standpoint."

Winwood sat down content in his probable defeat. The man from Hierophant stood up and thanked Winwood for his kind words before sharing his own.

"Libra, as you can tell by its representative today, is clearly a wonderful and respected house. I hear many stories of help they have given to people from all walks of life. But to be honest, they are so secretive in fact, that I am unable to divulge any more information than that I already have I'm afraid." With that the man sat down and waited anxiously for David's final decision.

David silently pondered his decision. He had never been so 50-50 about anything in his life. A split decision he would rather head down the middle of. Winwood had made Hierophant sound so appealing, yet his gut was telling him to go for Libra. Morally Hierophant was the better house and he wasn't in any danger with them, he wouldn't have to run away or hide or lie. But he also worried he would upset Winwood if he picked Hierophant. But then again, he was sure that Winwood would understand. Or would he? David's mind was all over the place. Six minutes and nineteen seconds of deep thought and his decision was made, he closed his eyes and after a deep breath he announced which clan he would be joining.

CHAPTER 13

SANE AS HOUSES

Helena gradually roused from her sleep; her deep blue eyes took their time to adapt to the bright white room. She tried to get up but was restricted and fell back into the mattress of a bed. She looked down to see a brown leather belt strapped across her mid region, Helena attempted to free herself before she realised her hands were also strapped down. She desperately tried to move her feet, but they were also pinned to the white cotton of the bed. Helena looked around the room in panic, she hoped to find something or someone that could help, there was nothing.

The room was white-washed with padded walls, even the door was covered. The only thing that wasn't white was the black metal bars barring the window, a camera in the corner of the room stood focused on her and the straps pinning her to the bed. She noticed her clothes had been replaced with greyish overalls, she presumed even they were white once upon a time, obviously faded from excessive washing. Helena struggled with her bonds again, this time putting her full effort into moving. But she couldn't. She screamed her frustration as loud as she could. After twenty minutes shouting she gave in. She then spent an hour sobbing, it was obvious nobody was coming to help.

Meanwhile, Mr Jewson was watching her on a monitor from his office with the door locked and his trousers undone, he loved new additions. Helena was so busy thinking about how she got here it didn't even occur to her that someone could be watching. The last thing she could remember was preparing lasagne. She remembered going through a bunch of holiday brochures but couldn't remember if that was before or after dinner. It must have been before she thought, because Tom wasn't there yet. When she thought of her husband it made her feel sick, she was repulsed by him, yet she had no idea why. Helena thought of something else just to escape the hurt she was feeling. She was scared and alone, and the only person she wanted to see made her feel physically sick.

After a while lying there with nothing else to do but look at the boring ceiling, a large clink at the door suddenly alerted Helena. It was a man in his fifties; he was overweight but smartly dressed with shirt and tie. He had matching brown trousers and a blazer. His bald head was sweating. His glasses filled up half of his face, they were clearly too big for him. He was carrying a clipboard and a newspaper in one hand and a pen in the other.

"Good morning Jennifer." A nervous-sounding voice asked. "Do you know who I am?"

"No sorry." She replied.

He almost smirked at her reaction.

"And my name isn't Jennifer." She angrily put in.

"Hmm." The man replied unfazed by her annoyance.

"Let me ask you a question Jennifer."

"I'm not Jennifer..." She shouted. She was sick of being called that already. "...Besides who are you? And what am I doing here?"

Helena tried to wriggle free. The man watched from behind with a smile. He went to touch her hair but changed his mind.

"What day is it?" The man asked, deliberately ignoring her questions.

She pondered for a moment before answering confidently. "Sixteenth of June."

"Okay." The man simply responded before writing something down on the clipboard paper.

"What! What are you writing down?" Helena shouted back. "Please." She added in a softer voice to change her tack, her angry approach clearly wasn't working.

The man liked the gesture, he put down his clipboard and began to undo the straps that bonded her arms with the bed. Helena winced slightly before realising she was being freed. Once her hands were free the man lunged for her midriff. She beat him to the belt buckle.

"I can manage thank you."

Jewson hovered in temptation before removing his hand from the area, as it hovered a bead of sweat dripped onto Helena's hand. She cringed but didn't move until he backed off. He watched fixatedly as Helena began to free herself. He looked like he had something to say but didn't know how to put it. By the time Helena began to undo the straps around her ankles, he had found his words and he didn't mince them.

"Being freed of your restraints is a good-will gesture, cross me and that good-will disappears. Do as you are told, and all will be well during your stay. Understand?"

"Perfectly." Helena scowled back.

The man picked up his clipboard and headed towards the door.

"Goodbye Jennifer." He said through a wry smile before he left and closed the door.

Helena waited until he was gone before calling him a jerk. She stretched out her frustration before jumping down from the bed. She noticed the man had left the newspaper. Helena was unsure if it was deliberate, but she picked it up to read it anyway. She looked down at the boring headline news about a politician's fumble on a plane. Then she noticed the date. Her mouth opened wide as she read it;

1st July 2017.

"What the fuck..." She said with such a shock that she dropped the newspaper to the floor. Over two weeks had passed.

"What the hell had happened? Why couldn't she remember it? Where was she? Where had the time gone? Why was the weird man calling her Jennifer?"

She questioned everything, including her own sanity, and that was exactly what Mr Jewson wanted as he watched her through the camera. He grinned as he watched her pacing the room. This time he didn't even lock his door, he knew nobody would dare come in without knocking first.

CHAPTER 14

A GRAVE DISCOVERY

Anthony was walking through streets he didn't know the name of. It was a grey kind of day, no sunshine, no rain. Not warm, nor cold, with just enough wind to lift the remaining sweet wrappers from the school run. Anthony had left home determined, but now he had no idea where he was going until he found himself at the cemetery where his best friend David Sixsmith was buried. He wasn't sure if he had come for answers or to pay respects, maybe both. He thought back to the funeral but all he got was painful memories and the location of David's gravestone. He headed towards it trying to think of something other than the pain of losing his best friend. Instead he chose to pretend David didn't exist. After all, guilt hurts a lot less than sorrow.

An old man distracted Anthony from his inner struggle, he was dressed in a grey beanie with a matching tracksuit bottom and top duo. He had mismatched gloves on, one red, one black. He looked like he was putting something on David's grave. It wasn't until Anthony got close that he realised it was grass seed. He was stamping in it as he went around in a circle. It irritated Anthony to the point he spoke out in anger.

"What ya doing?" Anthony bellowed from just a few yards away, shocking the man to the point he almost jumped into the air.

"Seeding. I've got to stamp it in or it won't grow." The man said as he increased his pace from slow to steady. It was only as Anthony got right up close that he realised there was barely a blade of grass on the grave, the mud covering it was dark and uneven. It looked as if David had been dug up.

"What happened here?" Anthony asked in a much softer voice.

The man finished what he was doing, grabbed a nearby spade and leaned against it before he answered.

"Well most graves sink a few days after the funeral, soon as a bit rain gets in and people walk over them and compact the soft soil and that, I'm guessing that's what's happened here."

"You're guessing?"

"Well this one was a right mess when I noticed it, soil all over the place. It's the third time I've topped it up now, and it's still not level.

"What does that mean?" Anthony asked in desperate hope.

The man had his full attention, he could have said a dragon did it, and Anthony would have believed him.

"I don't bloody know do I? Some kids messing about probably, or the crows have been at it, they keep bleeding pinching the seed anarl."

Anthony felt like a balloon that had been pumped up, just to be let go of and slowly deflate. He left without saying thank you and headed for the exit. Anthony went straight to David's house and stood opposite watching the house. Part of him hoped David would just suddenly walk out the front door, like this was all some sort of sick joke. After a while he began to feel dejected. He must have been stood there a good fifteen minutes when the front door eventually opened to reveal a smartly dressed man with a brown leather briefcase. Anthony instinctively hid behind a tree and continued to watch as the man glanced around suspiciously before getting into his white car and speeding away.

Anthony debated just going home and leaving it, but the intrigue was just too much. He walked over to the house and knocked on the door. He waited around a minute before knocking again. Eventually he heard footsteps before the door slowly crept open. It was David's dad Mike. He looked drunk, nothing Anthony was unaccustomed to, but what was weird was Mike just stood there, as if he did not recognise Anthony.

"Hi Mike, can I come in for a chat?" Anthony asked slowly.

A moment of realisation seemed to spread across Mike's face.

"Oh Anthony, come in." Mike said opening the door wider.

Anthony regretted it the second he entered. The smell of David's house was the first thing to hit him. A mixture of bleach, alcohol and sweet pea. The familiar smell nearly made him weep. The next thing he noticed was the quiet humming of Abba in the background, too quiet to enjoy, but just loud enough to figure out what song was playing. 'Chiquitita' from the 'Abba Gold' album. Next song would be 'Fernando'. He'd never liked the group personally but had been to David's often enough to know the album off by heart. They were a struggle to listen to now, because of the painful association.

Anthony followed Mike into the front room. David's mother Andrea was sat on the couch. She did not look up from the floor as Anthony entered the room and sat down. Mike sat down beside her and looked down at the exact same place on the floor as if forgetting about Anthony's presence.

"Who was that?" Anthony asked for the third time to no avail.

Anthony was really freaked out, then something suddenly clicked in his mind, David's webcam.

"I'm just getting one of my games." He lied before heading upstairs.

They didn't acknowledge him at all. They didn't even pull their heads up from the floor as he set up the webcam right in front of them peeking out from one of the many china plates that lined the room as decoration. He set up a connection through David's laptop to his own and pressed record. He wasn't sure what the hell was going on, but one thing was sure, Anthony was going to find out.

CHAPTER 15

CANNIBAL CAFE

"Libra." David proudly announced his decision.

Winwood positively beamed. It was the first clan trial he had won in a while. The judge banged his gavel with such a force that David almost fell from his chair.

"Very well. The decision has been made and is final. David Sixsmith will join the Libra clan for a minimum of fifty years. That is all. Next trial will begin after lunch." The judge announced before getting up and heading down the steps towards David.

"I wish you the best of luck." The judge said sticking out his hand for David to shake.

The judge then left the room as Winwood and the man from Hierophant both approached David with a smile.

"Good to have you on board." Winwood said patting David on the back.

The man from Hierophant gave a nod of acknowledgment that showed he wasn't disappointed, or surprised by David's decision.

"What now?" David asked from the ten thousand questions that had popped into his head.

"Follow me." Winwood said as he led David and the man from Hierophant out of the room. The speedy elevator back to the capitol building didn't seem too bad this time around. Maybe it was the excitement, or maybe David was finally adapting to the super-speed travel that the vampires used to get around. He hoped it was the latter.

A few hallways later and David recognised the man that stood waiting for them. It was Ryan, the human chauffeur for Libra.

"You joined us then?" Ryan shouted gleefully as the trio approached.

"Yeah… But it was a close one." Winwood voiced back trying to save the man from Hierophant any embarrassment.

Ryan jubilantly shook David's hand on arrival; he was clearly pleased to have David on board. David was buzzing from the reception; he had never felt so wanted in his vampire, or human life.

"How'd you get here?" David asked Ryan remembering he wasn't on the train.

"Drove." Ryan said with a smile.

"There's still another two trials to get through. You mind taking him for a coffee and filling him in a bit?" Winwood asked Ryan.

"Yeah no problem."

"I'm going for some lunch, then off to try and get some more people on board." Winwood declared pointing in the direction they had just come from.

"Cool. See you later then yeah?" David asked.

"Yeah. See ya." Winwood announced before walking off. "And I'd go for the squirrel syrup." Winwood shouted back before disappearing around a corner.

"What's does he mean?" David asked a smirking Ryan.

"You'll see." Ryan announced as they headed in the opposite direction.

Ryan walked so fast that David had no time to take in his surroundings as they moved from room to room, corridor to corridor. As the pace settled David found himself in what looked like a giant shopping centre. One he was unfamiliar with. The shops seemed so alien in their set up and not a single recognisable brand stood out from the dozens of shops they passed. Then David realised why. It was a vampire mall. David eventually picked up the strong scent of coffee as they finally entered one of the many shops. It was named Cannibal Cafe;

The heavy smell of blood and coffee lingered in the traditionally decorated cafe. The cosy looking seats, the newspaper littered tables and the frantic working till were all too familiar. He mused to himself how being a vampire wasn't all that dissimilar from being human, but the huge walled menu quickly made him realise how wrong he was.

Pick a drink!

Leech Latte £2, Bloodsucker Cappuccino £2, Mosquito Mocha £2, Espresso £2, Double Espresso £3, Frappe £2, Tick Tea £1.50, Parasite Hot Chocolate £2, Bottle of Still Blood £2, Bottle of Flavoured Blood £2, Bottle of Still Water £1.

Pick a blood shot - £1 extra!

Pig, Sheep, Cow, Rat, Squirrel, Chicken, Pigeon, Mixed Species, Artificial.

Add syrup – 50p!

Almond, Bubble-Gum, Hazelnut, Chocolate, Gingerbread, Caramel, Vanilla, Cinnamon, Mint, Peanut, Apple, Honey, Banana, Blackcurrant, Cherry, Cranberry, Strawberry, Mango, Pineapple, Raspberry.

Add a topping – 50p!

Chocolate sprinkles, Cream, Marshmallows, Blood foam, Cinnamon sprinkles.

David read the menu again and again trying to take each little element in.

"What does Artificial mean?" He immediately questioned Ryan.

"It's kind of the vegetarian option, not real haemoglobin."

"What would you like today sir?" Questioned a young vampire girl dressed in a blue t-shirt with Cannibal Cafe inked in red across the left of the chest. It looked like ordinary human work attire but the barista looked so young David wondered how old she was when she was turned. She looked no older than fourteen.

"One still water and a...?" Ryan answered turning to David.

"Erm...parasite hot chocolate with squirrel blood and erm... hazelnut syrup please."

"Do you want sprinkles and marshmallows with that Sir?" The worker asked.

"Yes please." David answered excitedly. Ryan was trying his best not to laugh at David's excitable nature. He paid for the drinks and the pair sat down at a nearby table.

"Why do you use human money?" David enquired as he watched Ryan put his change away in his denim jeans pocket.

"Easiness." Ryan simplified taking a sip of water before excitedly watching David with his drink. David grabbed a spoon and wolfed down all the marshmallows and sprinkles so he could get access to the hot liquid underneath. Once his route was clear he took his first sip. David eyes lit up as the full flavour of the coffee, squirrel and hazelnut blended together in his mouth. His taste buds positively bounced up and down with joy.

"That... is... amazing!" David pronounced as he desperately tried to cling on to the aftertaste that was vanishing down his throat. He forgot his environment a second and dived in for another taste getting foam and chocolate sprinkles all over his face. Ryan's laugh was audible outside the cafe. David was a little embarrassed, in fact no, he didn't care. The hot chocolate was amazing.

"How can you just settle for water?" David asked as he watched Ryan take another sip.

"Human remember?" Ryan answered with a smile.

David had totally forgotten.

"Oh yeah." David said with a laugh.

As he took another drink, he looked around the room. A nearby newspapers stand caught his attention. At first, he thought he saw the 'Sun' newspaper. But then his surprise turned to wonder as he noticed it was a vampire newspaper, and not the 'Sun' he mistook it for. It was aptly named 'The Shadow'. David couldn't help but smirk at its amusing consistency and name. The main headline stated that three vampires from the Trinity clan were still missing. A person took it from the stand so David couldn't read anymore. He instead moved his attention back to his coffee.

"So... anything about vamp life you wanna know about?" Ryan asked.

"Erm... How is it different from human life?"

"Well surprisingly not that different actually. We still get crime, financial problems. We still have accidents, relationships and so on. There are still companies buying other companies, vampire celebrities, vampire sports, vampire films, vampire music and as you just saw, we even have vampire newspapers.

"Why do you say 'we' if you're not a vampire?"

"Cos essentially, I am, and I'm not. The vampire world realises its need for humans and understands that total disguise from human knowledge is damn near impossible so it occasionally allows people, like me, to become citizens of its world." Ryan explained.

"Are they all chauffeurs like you?"

Ryan couldn't help but laugh. It was nice not being the new and naive member of the group anymore.

"No. There are three types of human citizens in the vampire world. The first is the donators which have a level one vampire passport, these are what the vamps call blood camels."

"Level one vampire passport?" David asked.

"Yes. They give blood and are paid for the privilege. But, they are restricted in where they can go, what they can know and so on. It's a risky business for both parties but a necessary one."

"Okay. What are the other two types of citizen?" David asked.

"The second is the contributors, or the 'blood help' the vamps call us."

"So, that's what you are?"

"Yeah. The contributors learn of the vampire existence, one way or another and have two options. Help out or keep schtum." Ryan informed.

"What access have you got?"

"I am allowed in all public areas like this and my clan's base, but where you've just been is classed as a government area, and its places like that, I can't go in."

David took another sip of his delicious coffee; the cup was almost empty by now.

"And the third type of citizen?"

"They are the deceptor's or blood sheaths."

"What do they do?"

"They help cover up vampire existence from humans, and can access most places including some places that normal vamps can't. But a lot of them use this privilege to break and bend laws, they're very shady characters and most of them end up as vamps anyway?" Ryan notified.

"So, there are quite a few humans allowed in the vampire world then?" David asked thinking about Anthony. If one thing could make this world a better place for him, it would be sharing it with his best friend.

"I'd guess a few thousand in every country, but it's very difficult to get an in. It takes a lot of luck to get near this world, especially with the deceptor's, and then you've got to have something damn useful to them. And you have to catch someone on a good day just to get a level one passport."

This news put a bit of a dampener on David's mood, but the return of Winwood was enough to distract him from it and they all left the cafe together. They walked for miles before David spoke again. He had a lot to take in.

"Where we headed?" He eventually asked as he grew bored of his own mind.

"A bed and breakfast." Winwood informed as he limped along the busy London streets. It was getting dark by now and they still had miles to go.

CHAPTER 16

PILLS AND POTIONS

Helena had been left to stew her memories and thoughts for nearly a full day before there was another knock at the door. The man that entered was a weedy kid who looked too young to be on work experience never mind employed; he had a blue uniform similar to a nurse's garb and was carting a tray full of medicine bottles, pills and sachets.

"Hi there, I'm Andy..." He said as Helena sat up on her bed.

Helena ignored it, she wasn't in the mood for guests but watched him intently nonetheless.

He looked over a clipboard and read the instructions aloud to himself so he wouldn't make another mistake.

"Room twelve, Jennifer White, one Zapanex, one Duloxetine." He stated before finding the relevant tablets and putting them in a small white paper cup

"My name isn't Jennifer, what are they?' She declared heading over towards him wanting a look at the clipboard.

He retreated a little as she moved towards him. She was surprised by his reaction but that didn't stop her.

"Chillax Andy. I just want a quick look." She assured before taking the clip-board from him.

She heard him mumble something about what she shouldn't be doing as she read down her profile. It was completely devoid of information, as if Helena didn't exist and she had started a new life as this Jennifer character. Her date of birth was miles out. It said she was diagnosed with schizophrenia aged twelve and had been in the asylum since she was eighteen. She thought she would test the information and clarify her sanity.

"How long have I been here now Andy? I was trying to think the other day, but I can't remember?"

Andy thought for a second before answering.

"It doesn't say in your file?" He asked trying to snatch back the clipboard. His attempt was weak, like a child.

"Obviously not." Helena announced handing it back to him and hoping he would take her word for it.

"I can't really remember." He answered as he ushered the cup of pills towards her. "Please take these."

Helena looked at the shaking cup. The nurse must have been terrified, he wasn't shaking when he first came in. Helena felt sorry for him.

"I will take your tablets, if you answer my question." Helena bargained.

"Okay, erm... it was about two weeks ago, but you were kept unconscious and fed through a tube until yesterday."

Helena snatched the cup and looked into it. One tablet was circular and white with a split through the middle, the top part had the letters CPN printed across it. The bottom half simply contained 100mg. The other tablet was a blue and yellow capsule. She couldn't see anything else on that one. Helena pursed the cup to her lips and strategically tilted the cup so the tablets fell to her tongue. Andy calmed as he noticed a swallowing action.

"What do they do?" She asked as she showed her tongue to prove they were gone.

"One's to help with your memory; the other is to keep you calm." He answered as he ticked her Monday box on the sheet. He looked at the time on his cheap watch and wrote that down too.

"Not long 'till you see your sister now." He casually noted.

"I don't have a sister." Helena declared before laughing. He was clearly delusional.

He looked down at her sheet. Jennifer's last name is White, Margaret's was Keen. Perhaps she was right.

"Oh, sorry my mistake, it's just you and Margaret look so alike."

"Who the hell is Margaret?" Helena asked.

"She's another one of our patients. Dinner should be about an hour. You will see what I mean then." The man finalised before wheeling his cart out of her room.

Immediately Helena turned her back to the camera and spat out the two soggy tablets into her hand. She wiped the milky residue on her trousers before walking over and sitting it the sun's rays that burned through her solitary window. Helena started to think about what Andy had said, the bit about having a sister. She was sure she never had one, but somehow it felt like he was telling the truth. She had the overwhelming feeling that her sister was the reason she was there in the first place.

Meanwhile, outside of Helena's room Mr Jewson pulled Andy over to one side of the corridor. The one blackspot of the hallway camera.

"Did she take them?" He hastily asked grabbing Andy by his uniform.

"Yeah." Andy fearfully replied.

"You saw her take them?" Mr Jewson questioned further.

"Yeah, I saw her swallow them both."

"Good." Mr Jewson added with an evil looking smile. He eventually eased his grip on the man.

"She doesn't seem that mad though sir." Andy sympathised.

"You just do as you're told, unless you want to share a cell with her..." Mr Jewson screeched as he gripped the man by the collar. He eventually let go attempting to un-crease Andy's work-wear with just his hands.

"...and she gets no food today" Jewson demanded before walking away.

CHAPTER 17

BACK TO BASE

The next morning David woke to unfamiliar settings. He was in a bedroom he didn't recognise. To the left and right of him were two unmade empty beds. David noticed the smell of bacon and sausages wafting through the air as he sat up. It made him instantly hungry. He washed himself in a nearby sink and his memories returned as he woke himself up. He was at a bed and breakfast. He remembered getting here and meeting a lovely human woman called Maude but not much else, certainly not going to bed. He put it down as tiredness and moved to find the cause of the fantastic smell that was sizzling in the air.

David heard chattering as he neared the source of the smell towards the back of the property. He pushed the door.

"Morning." Maude announced without turning away from her pans. It was as if she knew he was coming.

"Morning." He excitedly replied.

David's mother Andrea never cooked fry ups, in fact she barely cooked at all. The majority of his last meals as a human were takeaways and anything he could be bothered to make.

"Have a seat David." Maude announced as she began to plate up his feast of food.

David couldn't hide his smile as he was given a Full English Breakfast with all the trimmings;

Two fried eggs, two sausages, two bacon, two black pudding, (which was apparently a family vampire recipe that had been passed down the generations.) He also had one slice of fried bread, two slices of toast, two hash browns, fried mushrooms, one grilled tomato and beans. It must have taken some time preparing, but it was gone in minutes.

"Gosh, you lot must have been starving." Maude joked as she took everyone's plate away.

David, Ryan and Winwood sat contently silently until there was a knock at the door. Ryan stood up and pulled a knife from a sheath around his thigh, he slid it straight behind his back and backed up against a nearby cabinet of crockery. Winwood struggled up and ushered David towards the window, which would be their escape if things went sour.

"There's no need to panic, and you can put that away Ryan." Maude demanded as she headed towards the front door to meet the source of the knock. Ryan did as he was told but kept his hand near to it for quick access.

As Maude opened the door the trio stiffened up. In walked two bulky men, the first was dressed as a biker and had a scar from his right eye to the middle of his top lip. The other looked more like a teacher, dressed in a full suit and tie, with a long grey coat that hung down to his ankles. Maude closed the door behind the pair and led them through to the kitchen. They looked alert as they noticed the trio in the room.

"Vampires." The suited man said declaring the obvious.

"Not all of us, hunters." Ryan replied to get the facts straight.

David had never felt so awkward since becoming a vampire. He didn't know what was happening; he kept very still and silent for fear of starting something he didn't intend to. Maude didn't seem to know about the tenseness that was now in the room, or care. She simply filled up the kettle and got some new pans out ready to cook.

"We best be off now." Winwood stated before taking some money from his wallet and handing it to Maude.

"If you must." Maude declared taking the money and putting it in a utensil belt that was situated around her midriff. She began to count out change before Winwood hugged her as and told her to keep it. Ryan was next, he hugged her with one hand keeping his other free to go for the knife.

"It was nice to meet you by the way." Maude announced as she grabbed David and almost squeezed the life out of him. For an old woman, she was ridiculously strong.

"You too." David announced adjusting his newly-creased clothing.

"Well, see ya." Winwood announced as he turned his back ready to leave.

"See ya." The biker man joked back in a funny voice as he grabbed himself a seat.

Winwood stopped in his tracks in the hallway.

"Don't you dare Winwood, and you..." Maude announced grabbing the bikers hand and slapping him quite hard on the wrist. The sound echoed through the hallway, it had to hurt. Winwood left frustrated but he didn't dare disobey Maude. As Ryan and David left the house and turned a corner, they caught Winwood kicking over a bin, it was the first-time David had saw Winwood anything other than calm.

As they walked through the streets, back towards where David presumed Ryan had parked the car, David realised how much better his life was as a vampire. He couldn't even remember the last time he had had a fried breakfast, or really enjoyed a meal for that matter. David also enjoyed the little mysteries his circumstances occasionally now presented. The coffee, the fry-up, almost getting into a fight, it kept him on his toes, (even if he was bricking it at the time). He was also happy to be part of Libra, the only apprehension about it all was Chora, the woman that shot him. He wasn't looking forward to that reunion.

CHAPTER 18

POLICE STATION

Three days had passed and Anthony had the evidence he needed. The man with the briefcase was hypnotising David's parents and giving them some sort of chemical in their drinks. His instinct had told him to make multiple copies, one of which he was currently taking to the police station. He had never been to on before and it took him a while to figure out where the main entrance was. When he finally did, he burst through the automatic doors and shyly approached the desk.

Inside there was nobody manning the entrance. Anthony looked around to see an elderly woman sat at a group of seats going through a number of scraps of paper. He watched her for a few minutes, she seemed to be really struggling with the bits of paper as if they contained key moments of her life and she was putting them in date order.

Anthony was about to ask if she needed help when a cough from behind alerted him. He turned to see a woman was now at the desk dressed in the typical blue police uniform he had seen on TV so many times. She was really pretty, as if she was an actress playing a police officer. Anthony hesitated timidly before approaching the desk.

"Hi there." Anthony lamely said. His words were barely audible.

"Hi, can I help you?" She replied with a smile.

"Yeah I'd like to speak to the officer in charge of David Sixsmith's murder please." Anthony asked with a gulp.

"And your name please."

"Anthony Starkey."

"Okay give me a minute." She replied before disappearing.

Anthony had to wait at least ten minutes before the same woman returned, this time armed with a blue file, black pen, a notepad of paper and a tape recorder. She didn't say a word as she crossed the room and opened one of the doors at the side of the room, they looked like cells. Anthony was now unsure about the whole thing and wished he had just left it. For some reason, it was only now in this very moment that plausible ideas were occurring to him. What if the hypnotist was a police officer? Or just somebody trying to help David's parents with their grief. He wanted to go home.

"Anthony" The woman indicated while struggling to hold the door as well as all the other things that she was clinging to. Anthony knew it was too late to forget the whole thing. If he left now it would look so suspicious that he might even be considered a suspect, the only suspect as far as he was aware. He went into the room racing through other reasons he might be here.

"Sit down." The woman announced as she began placing things down on the table.

Anthony obliged without question as he looked around the room. The room and everything in it was cream, except the bulky black door that now kept him prisoner.

"Now, what can I help you with today Anthony." The woman asked. She was even prettier up close. She looked too nice to solve crimes and stop criminals. Her soft-spoken voice and beautiful face calmed Anthony a bit, who finally managed to regulate his breathing.

"Are you in charge of David Sixsmith's murder case?" Anthony asked when he had plucked up the courage.

"I'm Sergeant Rose Waters, I'm not in charge of the case no, but I am familiar with it and qualified to take and pass on any information you can give me today."

Anthony realised he was not obliged to give any information and it was perfectly acceptable to request information. He eased up and asked away.

"I was wondering where you are with David's case?'

"In what regards?" Rose asked slightly taken aback by his forwardness.

Anthony had to think about how he worded his question; he didn't want to give away what he had come for.

"Like, is there anything new?"

"I am not really allowed to discuss any details of his case, but I can say the case will probably be closed soon if no new evidence comes to light." Rose was very careful with her words, she wasn't lying, but she was trying to entice any information Anthony might have out of him.

"What! Why?"

"Well we have hit a wall I'm afraid, no evidence to help, no leads to go on. When this happens, an investigation is put to one side until we eventually uncover something new. For example, new evidence, witness testimonies, DNA. Basically, anything that could help with solving a case is usually enough to keep it open or re-open a closed case. You don't happen to have any such information, do you?" Rose knew he had a card up his sleeve. If he just wanted information he would of rang or emailed.

"But how can you find something new if you aren't looking?" Anthony responded with a slight frustration and anger in his tone.

"I am sorry, but there's nothing else we can do." Rose put back matching his tone. She stopped the recorder.

"So, you just put a weird doctor with the family and forget about it?" Anthony fumed. He had never been this angry his whole life. He got up ready to leave.

"What do you mean?"

"It doesn't matter." Anthony replied. He had gone from hot to cold in seconds. He just wanted to leave and approached the door ready to leave.

"What do you mean? Rose asked genuinely curious.

"I saw him coming out of David's house." Anthony had to fight back the tears filling in his eyes. His emotions were all over the place now. He turned his back to Rose just as a tear streamed down his face. He wiped it quickly with the sleeve of his hoodie.

Rose just sat there thinking to herself for what seemed like minutes. She looked confused.

"This man you saw. What makes you think he's a doctor? Can you describe him." Rose eventually asked.

"I saw him put medicine bottles into his briefcase after he left." Anthony lied.

"What type of briefcase?" Rose quickly asked, as if suddenly interested in what he had to say.

"It looked like a brown leather one, like one that people used to use in the olden days." Anthony remembered.

Rose seemed taken aback by his answer. She sat quiet for a while before getting up.

"Look a man with a briefcase isn't new evidence, but thank you for your time nonetheless." Rose indicated to the hallway as she opened the door for Anthony.

"If you don't mind, we have got other cases to look into." Rose put in. Her words were harsh and sharp and it didn't feel good saying them, but she needed to.

Anthony left the police station no further forward; in fact, he felt like he had taken a step back, he was so confused. As he walked home he realised his best friend was dead and he had to deal with it somehow and move on. Nothing he could do would bring back David.

Meanwhile, Rose checked the cubicles in the women's toilets to make sure nobody else was around. She unbuttoned a section of her top and put her hand inside her bra before pulling out a photograph. The photo was old and creased, it contained a man in a suit carrying a brown leather suitcase. It was the same man Anthony was talking about. Rose looked it at for a moment before whispering the words.

"Found you."

CHAPTER 19

FOOD FOR THOUGHT

It was day fifteen at the Shorebank Wellness Centre for Helena, at least she hoped it was. She had no way of telling for sure. Mr Jewson had brought her no more newspapers on his twice-daily visits. She had gotten used to his slimy demeanour and could even put up with the inappropriate touching. Which she suspected was all an attempt to get a reaction, one she wouldn't oblige, for now. One thing she couldn't stand though, was being called Jennifer. The more she was called it the more she believed in it. The more she believed in the name, the more she made up of her new life.

Helena had even begun to question whether she belonged in the asylum. Even more so as her real memories slowly returned to her. She remembered a daemon coming into her home and transporting her to her cheating husband Tom. Then bringing here, to the asylum, to break free a sister she never knew she had. Just because she remembered it didn't mean it was real. What was strange was there was no sign of the daemon that magically brought her here or the mystery sister she had been brought her to break free. Not yet at least.

The door to her cell suddenly opened causing her to stand to attention, tense and angry. She couldn't be bothered with Mr Jewson today, maybe this was the day she would stop him touching her for good. Her caution was unnecessary, it was Andy.

"Hiya, fancy a stretch and a bite to eat?" He asked politely.

"Yeah." Helena replied, she was so hungry at the thought of food she could eat literally anything. As she un-creased her straight-jacket and combed her hair with her fingers she didn't know what she was more excited about, the prospect of food or seeing beyond the four padded walls of her cell. She stood next to the door keen to head out like a dog about to go for his morning walk.

"Pills first Jennifer." Andy reminded.

Helena pretended to take her tablets and stood next to the door again.

Andy opened the door, it wasn't worth the anticipation. She left her padded cell to a hallway full of doors that no doubt led to more padded cells. Around twenty rooms lined the corridor, ten on each side. All of them were closed except number 3, Helena's. Her and Andy walked the corridor in silence. As they arrived at a set of big blue double-doors Andy opened one to reveal a massive cafeteria.

"You've got about an hour." He said after looking down at his cheap-looking watch.

As Andy began locking the door behind her Helena forced a question through a gap in the doors.

"Is my lookalike here?"

"I don't know." Andy answered forcing the doors closed before Helena could think up her next question. The first thing she did was remove the paste of tablet from her mouth, she disguised it with a cough and wiped it on the back of her dirty white overalls.

Helena turned to finally take-in the room she was in. The walls were coloured bright yellow with childlike murals all over them;

whoever had done them clearly hadn't been to art college. The Tinkerbell looked pregnant, Minnie the Mouse had the frame of an eight-foot body builder and Elsa from Frozen looked more like an old woman with long grey hair coming out of her hands. Helena giggled at their dreadfulness before looking at the rest of the room. In its centre sat four long grey tables lined with different sized and shaped seats, not a single one of the seats looked like they paired with the table.

Inside the cafeteria there was around twenty people, all of them girls. Only a few of them were sat in proper seats eating lunch like normal people should. In the corner of the room one girl was on her knees eating her dinner out of the tray like a dog. Another girl not far away from her had one hand against the wall and was stretching out with her fork trying to reach her tray of food on the floor. Helena pitied them, but the smell of sausages soon stole her attention, she didn't realise how hungry she was until she had smelled the food. Her tummy grumbled a loud embarrassing groan she was thankful nobody else noticed.

Helena grabbed a red tray and queued up behind a few people at a bunch of plastic fronted cabinets. She waited patiently until she found herself in front of two overweight women who were stood at the other side of the service area. Each was wearing a dirty green and white stripped apron and hat over the top of their normal clothes. She could smell them across the counter top. Helena didn't care, she had to eat something.

"What do you want?" One of the women grumpily asked.

Helena's response was sharp and genius.

"The usual please." She asked as nicely as she could. She bordered condescending.

"I've never seen you before in my life..." The woman answered before repeating herself. "...What do you want?"

Helena plumped for sausages, burgers and what looked like smash but the majority of her plate was filled with carrots. She walked and sat at the nearest seat with a grin on her face and the confirmation she needed. She didn't belong here and hadn't been here years as Mr Jewson had suggested. Now all she had to do was find her sister and a way out.

"Are you Helena?" A soft voice asked to the right of her as she began wolfing her food down.

CHAPTER 20

FAMILIAR SETTINGS

The forest was dim and eerily still when David and Winwood arrived and began strolling through its maze of foliage. It was raining and the smell of decomposing wood and putrid leaves lay stagnant in the air. A gust blustered around them as they moved towards the heart of the woodland. An assembly of organisms scurried away from their location as twigs snapped and moss squelched beneath their feet.

Winwood stopped David in his tracks to point out the entrance of the base. An old oak tree sat regally on its own, a good six-foot away from anything else. After a quick glance about, Winwood walked over to the tree putting his palm on the slimy bark. For a while there was no reaction, Winwood looked slightly confused before taking his hand from the tree, giving it a quick wipe on his trouser leg and then replacing it against the bark.

A few seconds later the lift shot-up into sight beside the tree shining fresh light into the darkened forest around them. David took two steps back, one in awe of its complexity and one out of shock. He knew what to expect but it still surprised him. They both walked into the lift area and he instinctively grabbed hold of the sidebar before it shot back down into the Libra base.

As the lift doors opened David instantly recognised the interior of the pale looking corridor, what he did not recognise or expect was to see several people standing there, shouting,

"SURPRISE!!!"

As the pair exited the lift. David looked around shocked. Banners lay strewn across the corridor. An abundance of distinct coloured balloons sat inflated against the ceiling and pinned to the walls. White tables sat neatly decorated to one side of the hall covered in a selection of food and drink. David glanced at Winwood with glee.

"Welcome to Libra." Winwood said with a wink.

Winwood managed to escape the encroaching crowd as it enveloped David. The onslaught of people either patted David on the back, hugged him or shook his hand.

As the sea of greeters dissipated David found himself face to face with the person he was least looking forward to meeting. It was the woman with long red hair who shot him a few days ago, Chora. She was dressed in a red Victorian style taffeta bodice that had a long black flowing skirt. She looked a lot prettier than when she had a gun pointed at him David thought to himself. She approached David cautiously as if she was scared of him.

"I'm sorry about the other day." She started before sticking out her hand to see if he would shake.

"Don't worry about it." David answered shaking her hand.

Both of them were eager to put the incident behind them as quickly as possible.

"Right well the food and drinks are over there, have a good night." Chora informed with a smile.

David quickly approached the food table with caution yet excitement, he hadn't eaten since Maude's lovely breakfast. He glanced at the plethora of foil plates that were filled with different types of sandwiches. Egg mayonnaise, tuna and cucumber, ham and pease pudding, then something he didn't recognise caught his attention before Doc come storming in.

"Ya alrigh' there laddy." Came Doc's raspy Scottish accent.

"Yeah, you?" Replied David.

"Aye, I'm good. Glad to have you on board." The Doc informed with a powerful pat on the back almost knocking David into the food.

"What's that?" David asked changing the subject; he pointed to a platter of sandwiches he didn't recognise. The bread looked like it had been soaked in something red like beetroot and it also looked like there was some sort of weird meat on top of it.

"It's what we call a bloody beef dip." The Doc answered before grabbing one.

It dripped over half the other plates of food before Doc managed to get it to his plate. Whoever placed it at the back of the buffet clearly hadn't thought it through. Doc took a small bite then began describing the sandwich with a full mouth of bread and beef.

"You cook the beef as normal but then dip it into some hot cow blood, you slap it into some bread while it's still warm and it soaks up all the flavour of the blood and the beef."

"Maybe try that another day." David said before plumping for a safer egg mayonnaise. He had enjoyed the blood coffee, but this just looked wrong. He watched Doc take another bite, blood spilled all over his plate underneath. Armed with only two egg mayonnaise sandwiches David looked around at what other food was available.

There were five bowls of cheeses ranging from pale yellow to orange. David plumped for the middle colour. Crisps, hot dogs, pickled onions, sausage rolls. His plate was filling nicely. A piece of pie and scotch egg later and his first plate-full was just about done. That's when he noticed a Tupperware dish full of what looked like nachos covered in a red and white sauce.

"What's that?" David asked Doc who was still cleaning his hands and face of blood with a tissue. He was so covered it looked like he'd had a nose bleed. He'd also gone through four napkins and counting.

"That's what we call Macho Nachos." Doc eventually replied with a grin.

"What's in it?" David asked intrigued.

"The white parts are a mixture of cheese, cream and chives, and mayonnaise. The red is a mixture of red pepper jelly, chilli, tomato sauce, and pigeon blood…"

"…It's nicer than it sounds or looks." Chora cut in as she began to grab some food from the table.

"I think I'll try some later thanks." David said as he glanced down at his overly-stacked plate. He grabbed one more egg mayonnaise sandwich and headed up the corridor to eat his food alone. He didn't want to be unsocial, but he didn't like eating in-front of other people. Unfortunately for him, the man who gave him the tour of the facility followed.

"You okay?" Trigger asked before taking a seat on the floor beside him. Getting comfy against the wall.

"Yeah thanks. You?" David replied eating the smallest thing on his plate so he didn't look ignorant. It took David a while to clear his plate as Trigger asked more questions than David knew what to do with. It was a good job he didn't get the bloody beef dip, it would have been cold by the time he got through it.

Without warning red bulbs started flashing in the hallway corridor above them. Everyone was tense and watched the lights as if expecting them to suddenly stop. It was so quiet David didn't dare break the silence to ask what the hell was happening. The alarm that followed would have drown him out anyway. The beep was deafening as it echoed through the base. It reminded David of a school fire alarm. Trigger got rid of his and David's plate into a nearby bin before returning to get David who was busy distracting himself from the noise by counting the bulbs that were flashing in the room. He counted eight.

"What is it?" David shouted through the wall of noise as Trigger returned. They were now both holding their hands to their ears to try and blot out the high-pitched sound.

"The silent red alarm means someone is in the woodland. This blasted noise means they are close to the entrance." Trigger shouted as he walked David towards a big red door. David hadn't even noticed it until now, and he definitely never saw inside during his tour. The blaring alarm quietened as Trigger closed the door behind them. David joined the group who were all standing around a huge computer surrounded by multiple video screens.

CHAPTER 21

ALARMED

Helena turned to see who had said her name. She was surprised and somewhat disappointed to find the girl who said it looked nothing like her. It wasn't her sister. It couldn't be.

"Who are you?" Helena asked. "...and how do you know my name?"

The girl smiled. Happy with the confirmation Helena had given.

"I'm Rachel. I'm friends with your sister."

Helena began to cry. This was the first bit of actual proof that she wasn't going mad. The daemon, the cheating husband, the sister, it was all true. After a minute or so Helena remembered her settings and looked up, she was surprised to see nobody was looking at her; everyone was busy making their own scene.

"How is she?" Helena asked before wiping her face dry with her sleeve.

"She's good, but she's in solitary." Rachel answered before nudging closer and putting an arm around Helena's shoulder to comfort her.

"How did she end up in there? And how do I get her out?"

"Jewson pushed Nicole too far?"

"Her name is Nicole?" Helena asked excitedly.

"Well, yes and no." Rachel said with a smile.

Helena thought she was getting to grips with her new reality, but every answer brought more questions. Rachel could see the confusion on her face.

"Nicole is a part of Margaret; they share the same body." Rachel tried to explain. She hoped Helena got it this time as this was getting increasingly difficult to explain.

"Like split personality?" Helena asked.

"In its simplest form, yeah sort of." Rachel finalised. Margaret and Nicole were entirely different people trapped in the same body, not personality constructs created by one person. But she couldn't be bothered to explain it any more today.

Suddenly a mighty alarm began sounding. Rachel gave a huge smile and got up. Helena seemed to be missing the point. She couldn't put the two and two together.

"This your doing?" Helena asked hopefully.

"They legally have to take us outside. Solitary or not." Rachel informed with a wink.

Helena half got the plan. She knew it would put both sisters outside together but couldn't work out how that would help, there would be more guards, and probably some sort or register involved.

"Care to fill me in with the rest of the plan?" Helena whispered as the guards and nurses huddled all the girls together in the cafeteria.

"This gets you both outside. You make a run for the outhouse towards the back of the asylum while a few of us distract the guards and run for the front. She knows you're coming for her. Once you're both together and out of sight that daemon friend of yours will come pick you up." Rachel whispered as they were ushered towards one of the emergency doors that had been opened.

"Wait. What about you?" Helena asked. She didn't have time to ask how she knew about the daemon. This was happening now.

"You can come get me later if you want." Rachel said with an unmistakable sadness to her tone. Deep down she knew she was stuck here, but this was the most fun she'd had in years.

As they all headed outside the girls were split into two different groups. One group that was acting orderly and another group that were acting in all sorts of peculiar ways. One girl had covered herself in food to avoid the noise and another was clapping really fast. They were getting roughed up and Helena felt sorry for them. She had never really seen anyone with a mental illness before, but she knew she had to keep her head in the game. She couldn't help them right now.

"Howd' you pull this off?" Helena whispered to Rachel as a nurse began cross checking to make sure everyone was there.

"I payed someone my dessert the other day to press the fire alarm when I gave her the signal. I didn't even think it would work to be honest." Rachel answered with a laugh.

Helena burst into kinks of laughter, until it started chucking it down with rain that was.

"Aw shit." Rachel irked as she felt the wall of rain. It was freezing cold. The guards seemed to revel in the fact the weather had taken a turn for the worse. They would get just as wet but they could easily change clothes, the girls would be stuck in their soggy overalls all day. As the patients began shivering Rachel knew they would be going back inside the building soon, but there was a problem; there was still no sign of Margaret. Rachel soon noticed Mr Jewson was also missing. She couldn't help but think he might be having one of his private moments with her. She had suffered two of these herself. The first time she was so high she didn't feel anything until the next day, but the second time she suffered every filthy undulating second of his greasiness.

CHAPTER 22

RED ALERT

As David got closer, he realised what he was looking at. It was a computer which was putting out information onto nine separate screens, set up in a three by three formation above. The screens showed every piece of information possible (from the woodland and the base.) They had a couple of screen dedicated to CCTV, there was temperature and vibration levels, a weapons and ammunition count, and a body count amongst other things. It was on this screen that David noticed one name that he did not recognise, Joel. Everyone else that was listed on the screen he knew and they were all present in that very room. Suddenly the alarm stopped sounding in the background and the red lights stopped flashing.

"Bloody hell man." Winwood stoked pushing his chair away from the mainframe computer.

People around him murmured, they were unsure why he had manually turned off the alarm.

"It's bloody Ryan." Winwood announced half frustrated, half relieved.

A fit of laughter filled the room.

"Who's Joel?" David unconfidently questioned.

The room fell into an awkward silence before Winwood got up from his seat.

"Someone let Ryan in and reset the alarm. I guess David still has someone to meet."

No-one verbally agreed to do it, but Winwood knew it was going to be done.

The walk along the corridor towards the back of the facility was a silent, long and awkward one. Part of him wished he hadn't said anything. At the end of the hall they reached a blank wall. David knew it was another secret door and he couldn't hide his smile;

"Azkaban Open." Winwood said with confidence.

A door shaped hole fell into the floor and revealed a series of steps leading downwards, David was grateful it hadn't revealed another lift. The pair descended in circles as the steps weaved round and down, their steps echoed their unmistakable arrival. As they reached level ground David was fascinated to see a huge room ahead of them, he gulped down a rising fear as he realised exactly what he was looking at, a jail. Ten wide cells stood either side of the chilly room. Only one was locked and Winwood led David towards it. They were soon stood face to face with Joel.

Joel's bright green pupils shone through his fluffy black hair and his matching gruff beard. His clothes were filled with little tares and creases; it looked like he had been fighting. On the floor beside the cell door stood an empty food tray.

"Joel, meet David." Winwood announced picking up the tray through a gap in the iron bars. He didn't take his eyes off Joel as he did it.

"Hi." David murmured, he was barely audible in the vast open space.

"David. That's a funny vampire name." Joel joked. His accent was Southern State American, his tartan shirt matched his accent.

Joel got up from the bed and moved further into the light revealing a face of cuts and bruises.

"He'll have a vamp name soon enough." Winwood announced. "How you doing Joel?"

"Bored as hell." Joel said turning his back to the pair. He looked up to where a window should be, there wasn't one.

"Well I did offer you some books." Winwood declared.

"I never was much of a reader, but I think I'll take you up on that offer of yours if it still stands. There's only so long a man can be left with his own mind before he changes it."

"No problem. What type you want?"

"Something fantasy. Just cos I'm stuck in here doesn't mean my mind has to be."

"I will send someone down with some food just now." Winwood said before turning around ready to leave, David quickly followed his lead. It was only as they neared the stairs that Joel seemed to notice, he was obviously deep in thought.

"Say hi to everyone for me." He shouted over to the pair.

"Bye Joel." Winwood yelled back, before he began climbing the stairs.

David followed and waited patiently until he was out of earshot of Joel.

"Why is he in there?"

"He killed people two people." Winwood announced as they got back upstairs. The entrance closed behind them and immediately began looking like a wall again.

"So, you're like the police, the courts and the jail then?" David asked struggling to keep up with Winwood as he limped away.

"No. We have a vampire court, but it's the judge, the jury and the executioner. Joel would meet his end there. Yes, he killed two people, but he claims it was self-defence. I don't think he should be killed for that. So, we are keeping him here for the time being. But David, under no circumstances should anybody outside this facility know about Joel."

"Okay, but wouldn't the courts understand if you told them everything?"

"No, and the circumstances of keeping somebody a secret in our base would be catastrophic to us all."

"Why do it then?" David asked intrigued.

Winwood stopped in his tracks, as if everything he had said to David up to this point was unimportant. His words were slow and serious.

"Sometimes in life you have to put others before yourself, no matter the consequences. Joel can't be trusted to be free, but that doesn't mean he deserves to die."

Winwood began walking again, he headed towards the rest of the group who had since left the control room and got back to sharing food, drink and conversation in the corridor.

"Are there other vampires like Joel? In his position, I mean?" David asked.

"Who said he was a vamp?" Winwood replied with a grin.

"Wait, then what?"

Winwood began to walk away before muttering one word back to David.

"Werewolf."

David stood there in shock as Winwood walked away. Ryan and Doc came over and chatted for a while but David didn't hear a word of it.

CHAPTER 23

EXIT STRATEGY

Rachel was pleased to see Mr Jewson come out into the courtyard after a few minutes; Helena was less pleased to see his face. (Although she was aware his presence was good news for her sister.) A fire crew soon arrived and were just as quickly dismissed. It was obviously a prank, but the asylum girls enjoyed every single second of their view while it lasted.

Mr Jewson was currently a shade of beetroot he was so angry. He was angry he had to get up, even angrier he had to leave the premises in the rain, but the thing that irritated him the most, was that some people thought that they had more authority than him. Jewson loved being in charge more than he loved his whisky, and the way the fire crew were going on made him want to drug the lot of them. Even he knew he would never get away with it, his revenge on them would have to wait. He impatiently waited until the fire crew were out of earshot, then he took his frustration out on his staff, who in turn took it out on the patients. The whole group were manhandled back inside while Mr Jewson turned the air blue behind them.

"Thanks Ems." Rachel said as she walked past the culprit.

"It was worth it just for the firemen." Emma said with a wink as the group were escorted back towards their cells. Spirits were unusually high despite the way the girls were now being roughed about, it was as if they had been on some exciting excursion for the day and nothing could kill their buzz. It was good to see for the few honest guards that worked the wards, Andy included.

"Do we have a plan B?" Helena whispered to Rachel before they were split up.

"Not yet." Rachel shouted back before she was thrown into her cell.

Helena managed to stay on her feet as she was pushed into her cell. She was rewarded with a kick to the midriff, it was an unwarranted bonus from one of the guards who thought she looked too happy. He was about to give her another one when Andy pulled him away.

"Let's get them away quick. Give Jewson a chance to cool down."

The guard threw Andy's arm away but obliged and locked Helena in. She was so winded it took her a while to realise there was someone else in the cell with her.

"You." She said as she noticed his face. "Please."

"Don't worry I will get you out." The man said offering her his hand and helping her up. It was the daemon Elathan.

"Let's go now; I don't think I can take another second of this place." Helena said lying on the bed in the foetal position, it hurt less there.

"How about another day?" The man asked. The question was rhetorical.

"If you can manage to get your sister in here with you tomorrow at seven pm exactly. I will get you both out of here. It can't be any other time though." Elathan's words were slow and precise. This wasn't a request; it was an order.

"There's three of us going." Helena words were equally demanding.

"Sorry that's impossible. I'm not even sure I'm strong enough to get the two of you out, never mind three."

Elathan words were sympathetic and honest.

"Then don't bother, if you're too weak. I'm not leaving without Rachel." Helena sat up through the pain to show she was serious. "I will get us all out another way."

Elathan looked at Helena like she had put him in an awkward position, for a while neither of them said anything.

"I can't make promises for her, but I will try. Make sure all three of you are here at seven." Helena went to ask another question but it was too late, he was gone. He had disappeared into thin air again, but this time he left something behind, hope.

Helena slept straight through the night and most of the next day. She was eventually awakened by a knock on her cell door, she knew this meant she had to pretend to take her medicine again. It was amazing how stupid the guards were. Although she realised it was probably a lack of care, rather than a lack of brain cells. She hoped it would be Andy doing the medication round so she could thank him for his kindness the day before. He was a good man; one she would like to have met in different circumstances. Her hopes were disappointed by the appearance of a rotund man she had never noticed before.

When the nurse eventually went, she found herself grateful that it wasn't the man that kicked her, or Mr Jewson. She wanted revenge on them both, but she wouldn't risk it for a chance to escape. Maybe one day she would return. Helena found it hard to look into the future, it was so unclear. She couldn't guess the next hour of her life, never mind a week away. It was just as hard to look back, the cheating husband and the life that reminded her of him. At the same time, she missed it, she missed him. Helena looked up at the clock that was imbedded in her cell wall. It was so high she could barely make out the time. It was strategically placed, too high for somebody to get it and use the parts of the clock against the guards or themselves, but it was also there so the patients could watch their life tick away. It was 2.15pm. Helena still hadn't had lunch, and she hadn't heard any cell doors open since the medication run. She began to worry.

It was 4pm before she decided to do something about it. She banged on her cell door so hard that the hallway watchman couldn't ignore it any longer. When she asked about dinner she was cited one word only.

"Punishment."

When she asked if he would send a message for her, she was kindly given two more.

"Fuck off."

After an expletive laden tantrum, she realised she only had three hours left to come up with a plan, or potentially be stuck in the asylum forever.

CHAPTER 24

BEING FOLLOWED

Anthony was at college in the middle of an IT lesson. He was struggling to swallow the hurt that parched at his throat. The empty seat beside him was a stark reminder of his recent loss. He painstakingly looked around the room for some off chance that David was sitting elsewhere. As his gaze passed a hallway window he noticed a woman looking in at him. She caught his gazing eyes and disappeared with a sharpness that was deliberate. Anthony had an urge to go after her but decided against disturbing the rest of the class. Several minutes later his lesson finished anyway. He hastily stuffed his work away and rushed outside but whoever it was, she was gone.

Anthony dismissed it and headed towards the college cafe. Over by two vending machines, he emptied his pockets and raked through the change in his in ink-laden palms. He sat at the nearest table with his coffee and crisps. As he began munching through the contents of the packet he noticed a woman enter the cafe and look around. It was the same girl who was watching him in his lesson. Now that he had more time to reflect her facial features he soon realised that he recognised her, but could not immediately recollect where from.

He left his breakfast idle and approached her quickly. As she spotted him, she left the room. Desperate not to lose her again he sped up after her, almost knocking people to the floor as he stormed out through the cafeteria doors. Outside he was met with crowds of people and beaming sunshine; he squinted around hopefully, almost to the point of panic. Finally, he spotted her heading towards a football field and persisted after her. He finally closed in on her, before realising who it was.

"Why are you following me?"

"Do you remember me?" She asked him clearly ignoring his question.

"Yes. The police woman? What do you want?"

There was an obvious pause. She was thinking about how to word the question.

"The man, with the briefcase. Did you get a good look at him?" She eventually asked.

"Yes why?"

"Is this him?" She said pulling out a scuffed photograph from her hoodie pocket and handing it to him.

Anthony looked at it, the man in the photograph was the same man he saw leaving David's house, he was dressed identically with the same briefcase in hand. It was the same person.

"Yeah that's him." Anthony stated handing the photograph back. "But why have you got a photo of him, and what's this about?"

"That photo was taken in nineteen-ninety-nine, when I was fifteen." Rose mentioned before putting the photo away in her pocket.

"What's your point?" Anthony demanded.

"Well he hasn't aged a day, has he?" Rose noted.

"So, he's got a good face cream, I still don't get why you've followed me. Am I in trouble?" Anthony asked.

There was a long pause while Rose thought out her words.

"Because the year that photo was taken was the year my sister Daisy went missing." Rose said trying to hide her face.

"I'm sorry to hear that, but I still don't understand." Anthony sympathised.

"Well we were all busy looking for her 'till he showed up!" Rose began before wiping a single tear from her face. "Soon after his visits, my parents stopped looking, as well as the police."

"That's pretty weird." Anthony stated.

Anthony thought about David's parents. He suspected they were being hypnotised but he thought it was more wild hope than fact. Maybe his hunch was correct.

"Has he ever spoken to you, or tried to convince you that your friend won't be found?" Rose asked struggling to compose herself.

"No but Mike and Andrea, David's Mam and Dad. Well, they've just about give in."

"It's the man with the briefcase." Rose affirmed. "I don't know how he does it but he convinces people to give up their hope."

"The bastard." Anthony spat out. You could tell he rarely swore by the way he flinched at his own words. Like they were poison on his tongue.

"But the question is, what are we gonna do about it?" Rose asked simply.

"What are you proposing?"

"First job is to find out who our mystery man is, and what he's up to. Then find out what he's done to Daisy and David."

Anthony wasn't sure where this new road would take him, but he was happy to be on it. He finally had optimism that he could actually find his friend David. Dead or alive he was going to get to the bottom of this whole thing.

CHAPTER 25

FIRST TIME

With their accelerated healing, it was hard for a vampire to get drunk, or wake up hungover, but somehow David had managed both. It was probably the rate at which people were plying him with booze that did it. Everyone wanted him to quaff their favourite alcoholic drink and David was too nice to refuse. He even tried some of Doc's Firebrand Whisky, a mature spirit with the kick of a dragon. The blend of cinnamon and spices still evident in his mouth as he awoke. David got up and drank from the blood dispenser like it was second nature now and after several cup-fulls he began to feel rejuvenated. After a stretch and a yawn, he noticed the fresh set of clothes lying on a nearby seat, a new looking tracksuit combo and some trainers.

After getting showered and changed he left his room in search of someone. He was halfway through the corridor when he picked up the sound of grunting. Unable to work out whom or what it was, he followed it. The sound directed him to the combat and training room. He knocked and entered. Chora, Legitus, Trigger and Torus were standing in the middle of the room looking rather clammy in their gym gear. Legitus looked completely out of place without his usual waistcoat and trouser ensemble. They stopped whatever it was they were doing as David entered the room.

"Morning." The grouped shouted over at him.

"Morning, what are you doing?" David asked.

"Training. We didn't wake you, did we?" Doc asked from the corner of the room. There wasn't an ounce of sweat on him, he was clearly observing.

"Some of us need it more than others." Torus joked.

"Training for what?" David asked getting closer. He was intrigued.

"The work we do is extremely dangerous. We need to be fit, and be able to fight." Legitus added before lunging a sneaky punch towards Torus. He blocked it with ease as if he was expecting it. He also managed to block Chora's lunging kick and jump out of the way of Trigger's leg swipe.

"Watch for now, then you can join in." Torus said before blocking three more strikes from Legitus.

Once David backed away the trio went after Torus with ferocity.

"Why three on one?" David asked Doc as the fighting went full speed in front of him

"You'll see." Doc answered, his eyes glued on the fight.

David watched as Trigger, Legitus and Chora took turns trying to hit Torus, but they struggled to get near him. The few strikes they managed to connect looked like they had no effect at all. It wasn't long until Legitus was pushed out of matted area onto the hardwood floor. He decided against getting back up. Chora seemed the quicker of the three but it wasn't long until she tapped herself out of a submission hold. Trigger was left one-on-one and he didn't look happy about it. He changed his stance to defensive but struggled to block the combo of attacks that were launched at him. After taking several strikes to his body Trigger bowed his defeat and tried to catch his breath.

"You want a go?" Torus said with a smile to David.

"I'd like to just start with the basics if that's okay?" David tried.

"How basic, you know how to throw a punch right?" Torus joked.

"Erm. Actually no..." David said honestly. "...I've never actually been in a fight before."

After everyone had caught their breath and drank some water the training began for David. He learned several attacks and several blocks and was forced to switch between them, they started slow but by the afternoon he was going so fast he had worked up a sweat. It wasn't until he was showering before dinner that he realised how much his shins and arms hurt from the repeated parries. All of his muscles ached, even the ones he didn't know he had. As he began to get dressed he noticed there was a blue light flashing in the room. He worried about how long that had been happening without him noticing. He quickly finished getting ready and went in search of some answers.

Eventually he bumped into Trigger who was waiting outside the meeting room for him. As David approached Trigger spoke.

"FYI, blue light just means a meeting has been called."

"Sorry I didn't know..." David began apologising.

"Don't worry about it." Trigger said with a slap on the back as they both entered the room.

David found a space between Doc and Chora at the black glass table that sat central to the room. As he and Trigger both took their seats he noticed Winwood, Ryan, Torus and Paige were also present. A noticeable absentee was Joel. David felt sorry for him and hoped he got that book he was after. When everybody was sat down and quiet, Winwood began.

"Right people we have received a missing person's report." Winwood began.

An image popped up on a whiteboard screen to show a man with an unkempt stubble. He looked normal.

"This is Mr Pearce. Just over two weeks ago, his wife appeared at his place of work, out of nowhere, then just as suddenly disappeared from the room and hasn't been seen since." Winwood informed.

A photo of his wife appeared on the screen. She had bleach blonde hair and deep blue eyes.

"He believes there may have been another man in the room at the time but cannot confirm this for sure." Winwood added.

"Any description on the other man?" Torus asked.

"He said it happened so fast that he didn't get a proper look at him." Winwood answered.

"Any other witnesses?" Chora asked.

"Yes actually, his boss, a..." Winwood looked down at a piece of paper on the table. "...A Mrs Groves, and she confirms his story."

The group looked disappointed and surprised; as if all of their theories had been disproved in one fell swoop. David didn't have a clue what this meant or what was happening, but he was loving every second of it. By this point he was sat upright with his ears pricked to make sure he heard everything, like some sort of school swat.

"Any theories?" Winwood asked the group.

Winwood waited, nobody replied. It was obvious none of them liked guessing incorrectly.

"Okay so I wanna go down three different roots with this investigation. Firstly, I want an interview on Mr Pearce and Mrs Groves, if both stories match up we can possibly rule them both out. Myself, Legitus and Chora will be going down that route." Winwood dictated.

David could barely hold his excitement; he was almost bobbing up and down at the thought of what job he might be given.

"The second route I wanna go down, is an investigation of the Pearce household. We should be able to rule out magick, daemons, haunting and human kidnap from that side of things. Torus, Trig and Ryan, I want you guys there." Winwood said before handing over a bunch of papers to Torus.

"Finally, Paige and Doc I want you to stay here with David. Show him the computer system, teach him the basics of an investigation from the ground up."

David wasn't too animated about staying in the base, but he was more than willing to follow orders. As each group left the base for their different assignments David wished he was going with one of them, any of them. Instead he followed Paige to the library trying his best not to show his disappointment.

As he entered the massive library he realised he didn't have it so bad. David loved learning and by staying in the base he wasn't in any danger. David looked in awe at the gigantic room before taking a seat with Paige at one of the computers central to the room. Paige started by showing him a program called the Creature Feature Program (CFP for short). It contained information on all the world's creatures and what they were capable of. Paige showed David how to input information and therefore narrow the search. With not much information to go on they were still left with a bunch of different creatures. David read down the list with amazement. Human, Vampire, Werewolf, Angel, Demon, Warlock/Witch, Gods, Genies...

"These are all real?" David asked excitedly.

"Yep." Paige said with a smile. She had never seen anybody so excited about her computer program.

Paige clicked the first box, human.

"When you click each creature box, it brings up area populous, missing and wanted people, creature traits, identification techniques, strengths, weaknesses and so on. Our job today is to get a list of potentials that can hopefully be whittled down some more when the team return with more information." Paige conveyed before moving over to a separate table, she grabbed a huge red leather-bound book and sat down reading.

David felt like he had been given a toy to play with to keep him out of her hair while she worked. He didn't mind though, it was an interesting toy. David clicked about and read little bits of information as he familiarised himself with the program. He was surprised however when he looked up at the clock and five hours had gone by.

CHAPTER 26

TIME IS RUNNING OUT

It was 18:54, when a bang on the door distracted Helena enough to look away from the clock. She wasn't even paying attention to the time, just watching her life tick away. But now that she registered the time, she began to panic. She had six minutes to get her sister and Rachel into her cell. She didn't even have a plan. The bang was much louder the second-time round. She walked towards the door with a lame "Hello?" But there was no answer. She pulled on the door handle fully expecting it still to be locked, but it swung open to reveal three people. Rachel held Andy in a headlock with one hand; she had his keys held to his neck like a blade with the other.

"Howdy partner." Rachel beamed before barging into the room. Margaret, Helena's sister, silently followed her in.

It was a strange moment for Helena, it was like looking in a mirror but someone changing little elements so the person staring back wasn't quite the same. Like two artists who had painted the same image differently. Margaret had the same blue eyes, the same noise, same ears, even the same mouth. But her hair was a lovely deep ginger, Helena was a tad jealous.

"Quick take his trousers off." Rachel announced.

For a second Helena was mystified, she was thankful when Rachel provided her the reason.

"We need his keys; they're stuck to his lanyard."

Andy didn't know whether to be turned on, or scared, as the girls ripped his trousers off. He settled for both. Yet he was grateful when they chucked him out the cell and locked the door behind him. Helena felt sorry for him, but this was a necessary evil. She looked up at the clock. It was 18.57. Three minutes left.

"How did you...?" Helena started.

"...Your friend Elathan." Rachel cut in trying to catch her breath.

A few moments later, shouting could be heard in the hallway outside. The voice unmistakable. The girls confirmed in unison.

"Jewson!"

As keys jingled on the other side of the door, Helena and Rachel instinctively ran for it. They made the door just as it was opened and managed to force it closed. The guards forced the girls back a little, but they managed to shut it again. With no way to lock it from the inside the girls were forced to rely on their strength keeping the door shut, but it wasn't holding.

"Margaret help." Helena pleaded as she felt the door being forced open.

Margaret just stood there looking confused as the door opened wider.

"Margaret!" Helena shouted.

Margaret continued to just stand there looking at the wall as if she was daydreaming. Then, as if she had just woken up Helena's sister ran over and pushed the door. The three of them had the strength to close it and hold it shut.

"Sorry sis, Mag's a bit slow sometimes." Came a confident voice from Margaret's mouth, but it wasn't her. In fact, her whole persona had changed. Helena expected to meet Margaret's other side at some point, but she did not expect such a drastic shift in personality. It was like two completely separate people.

"Bout time Nicole." Rachel said with a smile through her gritted teeth.

Helena took one step back and looked up at the time, it was 18.59. She pushed back against the door with everything she had, knowing she knew she had done it, she had escaped the asylum. With nobody on the other side of the door it swung open and everybody pushing fell inside. As they got up they looked around bewildered, the girls were gone. Mr Jewson's impatience eventually got the better of him and he burst through them like a Rugby player.

"What happened? Where are they?" He bellowed, looking around the room as if the guards hadn't already done so. He stormed around pushing walls and lifting up pillows to make sure there was no sign of the girls. Jewson checked every inch of the floor before looking up at the ceiling.

"Well get me some fucking ladders." He shouted, forcing veins through the skin of his forehead. Nobody had ever escaped his clutches before and he wasn't ready to accept defeat just yet.

"I will get you Helena, mark my words."

CHAPTER 27

NIGHT-TIME INVESTIGATION

Winwood, Legitus and Chora arrived at ramshackle building disguised as an expensive hotel. Helena's husband Tom Pearce had decided to stay there (now that he was armed with a fear of his own home.) Legitus approached the front desk and requested Tom's attendance in the nearby hotel bar. The trio were sat with their second drink by the time a dishevelled-looking Tom arrived. He looked tense and approached the group with caution.

"Who are you? What d'ya want?" Tom demanded.

"Hi Tom, my name is William, I am from a branch of the police force that investigates unusual cases. These are my fellow officers." Winwood convincingly lied.

Tom Pearce sat beside them but did not utter a word. Eventually bored with the silence Winwood spoke again.

"What happened on the night of the ninth of June Tom?"

"I already told a bunch of your friends who didn't believe me, and arrested me for the trouble. I only got out because I had an alibi." Tom rallied, he was clearly infuriated.

"We are a completely different department from the people you spoke to before. We don't like them much either." Legitus tried to sympathise.

"Ok. But you won't believe me." Tom mused.

"Just try us." Winwood convinced.

"Ok. So, I was in my office... working, when my wife suddenly showed up and shouted at me for working late. But then she stormed off. As I went after her, that's when I saw him. Some man just sitting there on a desk, dressed to the nines looking pleased as punch. He looked like a tool in my opinion. So, my wife just walks towards him and they both bloody disappear into thin air."

There was a pause as the group pondered further questions.

"How did they disappear?" Legitus asked.

"What do you mean how did they disappear? They were there, then they weren't. I dinno how they did it."

Tom stood up frustrated.

"Yeah but did they did just become invisible, did they slowly fade out, did they turn to smoke or what?" Legitus explained his question more carefully.

"Look I don't know who you are, but asking me stupid fucking questions isn't going to help me find my wife." Tom yelled before storming out of sight.

After Tom left, the trio drank the last of their drinks before leaving.

"Well that didn't help." Chora noted as they walked up the busy street away from the hotel.

"Actually, it did." Winwood informed.

"How?"

"Cos, we now know he was having an affair." Winwood said with a smile.

"Obviously, but how does that help?" Chora asked.

"Because it's probably some kind of fabrication for attention." Winwood dismissed.

"Fair enough. Case closed?" Legitus asked.

"For us I think, yeah." Winwood confirmed.

*****

Meanwhile Torus, Trigger and Ryan had been sitting in a car outside of Mr and Mrs Pearce's home for a few hours now. Nothing had happened out of the ordinary. They decided they would have one quick look around the building and inside, then head back to the base. Torus and Trigger grabbed some stuff from the boot of the car while Ryan kept watch. Torus started clockwise with an EMF detector looking for residual spikes left by ghosts or daemons. Trigger chose an infra-red camera to look for heat signatures and began walking anti-clockwise. Neither had wielded any results when they passed each other at the back of the property or as they both came back around to the front door.

"Whose turn is it to pick it?" Trigger asked removing a lock-picking tool from his pocket.

"Rock, Paper, Scissors?" Torus asked.

They both put a fist out and counted to three, throwing a shape out on the third count. Trigger won with scissors.

"Be quick." Trigger said passing Torus the lock-picking tool.

Torus put down the EMF and began unlocking the door while on his knees. He had it open within a minute. Once the door swung open he grabbed his EMF and went upstairs, while Trigger checked downstairs with the infra-red camera. Trigger started in the kitchen and began working back towards the front door. As he scanned past the window he noticed the windowsill was as black as sin. Something cold had been there, he moved in for a closer look. It was evident upon further inspection that something had been sitting there, something definitely not human.

"Torus. Come down here." Trigger shouted up before having a quick scan of the rest of the room to make sure whatever was there before, wasn't there anymore. Torus bounded down the stairs intrigued. He had found nothing upstairs.

"Scan the windowsill." Trigger asked doing another speedy check of the room just to make sure.

As Torus hovered the EMF scanner over the windowsill it went berserk, lighting up its full-beam red as it beeped rapidly. Something was definitely there at some point. Torus scanned the rest of the room, but there weren't any other results. Whatever was in the room had pretty much sat on that windowsill for the majority of the time that they were there.

"Well there was definitely something supernatural here." Torus announced as they left the house and closed the door behind them so that it re-locked.

"What should we do?" Trigger asked as they got back into the car.

"Take us to Priveam Ryan, I want to ask Celeste a few questions then we will head back to the base and fill Winwood in with what we have found." Torus announced before the car drove off.

*****

David had been using computers and books to investigate this case for the whole day and was beginning to get a little tired. He had learnt so much about the world he couldn't comprehend how the human world lived so oblivious to what was happening around them, like he had done so, for so many years. David thought about his friend Anthony and wondered if he had ever seen something that couldn't be explained, something supernatural. He thought about his parents and wondered if they had ever seen anything. As he sat and thought about his only friend and his family, he realised how much he missed them. His parents weren't the best, but they were the only ones he had. Just then he heard talking in the hallway and realised that Winwood, Legitus and Chora had returned. He wiped his face clear of tears and headed out into the hallway to greet them.

CHAPTER 28

EXISTENCE

Anthony and Rose were sat watching David's house from Rose's car, just twenty yards away. The man with the briefcase had been in there for one hour and twenty-seven minutes. They had gone through two packets of mint imperials, and almost ran out of things to talk about when he finally did emerge. The pair instinctively ducked out of sight as he glanced up and down the street.

They both remerged from behind the dashboard as his car pulled away. Rose's started up her rusty white Polo, spun it around and drove off in pursuit. They followed his car along a tonne of streets before he eventually pulled into an industrial estate. Rose parked several feet away, with a car in-between the pair. She turned off the engine and pulled out her mobile phone, pretending to speak into it. Anthony noticed he had his briefcase as he passed them both on his way towards a bar.

Rose watched him enter it through her wing mirror.

"What do we do now?" Anthony asked.

"I don't know." Rose answered.

She wanted to wait for him to come back out, but every second he was in there, could have been another second he was getting away. She lasted a few minutes, and then she couldn't take the anticipation.

"I'm going in." She said removing her seat beat and getting out.

"Wait." Anthony said quickly following her out.

Rose thought for a moment before going into her pocket and removing a little pad of paper with a pen attached to the side. She wrote something down before ripping it from the pad, folding it and handing it to Anthony.

"If shit goes down, I want you to get out and go to this address. Tell him he was right and the rose has wilted."

"What does that even mean?" Anthony said taking the paper and putting it in his back pocket.

"Just do it. Now. We are a couple. We met three year ago, first date Pizza Hut, I love reality TV, but I hate action films." Rose said before linking his arm and dragging him towards the bar.

Anthony felt uncomfortably shy but pleasurably excited at the same time.

As they entered the bar the smell of stale lager and furnished wood immediately ruminated in their nostrils. They were surprised to find the bar was quite busy. Three men sat in aisles, one man was stood behind the bar and another sat at the bar counter, with a briefcase resting against his stool. He didn't look up as they entered, but everyone else did. Rose quickly grabbed Anthony's hand by his fingers. Although her touch was cold and soft, it made Anthony feel warm.

Rose gave a gentle pull towards the bar and Anthony followed. As they neared the bar they noticed a single word projected beneath an archway. The word *'Priveam'* dominated in red spray paint. The letters had dripped and dried like blood on the wall. Almost everything in there was some shade of red to match the paint. Ivy and Roses filled up most of the walls. Crosses and pentagrams enclosed what was left, it was definitely gothic in design. They cautiously approached the heavily tattooed barman as he finished pouring a drink for the man with the briefcase.

"What can I get you?" He asked with a smile as if he knew something they didn't.

"A pint of lager, and an orange J-Two-O please." Rose demanded smiling at Anthony.

Anthony was bricking it, he tried to force a smile through the fear but it never prevailed. He hoped the alcohol he wasn't used to drinking, would give him the courage he wasn't used to feeling. As the barman served their drinks the man they had followed here downed his, got up and walked off. Rose didn't want to make it obvious that he was the only reason she was there. She was glad he had left his briefcase behind, it was a good excuse to look back. Part of her wished she hadn't turned around as she watched him lock the entrance to the pub from the inside. As the lock rattled in place the three men in the aisles all stood to attention.

Rose wasn't stupid. She hadn't come without preparation, she quickly let go of Anthony's hand to pull out her stolen Glock 17, a standard police issue. She pointed it at the man they had followed here. The man seemed unfazed by the brandished weapon pointed directly at him.

"And who might you be then?" He asked with a grin painted across his face.

Rose was surprised he had the illusion of being in control. She had the gun.

"Remember what I told you." Rose quietly asked Anthony. He didn't dare turn around and simply watched the barman block his exit the other way.

"Yeah." Anthony squeaked.

"Ah come on. If you're going to kill me at least tell me your name." The man said taking a sip of one of his friend's pints.

"You first." Rose demanded moving the barrel from person to person to stop any sudden moves.

"My name is Cerevad, I presume you're a pair of amateur hunters. No?" The man questioned.

"Hunters?" Rose queried. She was confused.

"You're not even vampire hunters..." The man positively giggled. "...even better..."

The other vampires in the room just looked at him as if expecting an order.

"...Well get on with it." He added with an urgent flick of his wrists before he sat down with his pint to watch it all enfold.

One of the vamps ran straight at Rose.

"Freeze." She shouted as he neared her.

She dropped the aim of the gun towards the legs of the nearest man. She took a deep breath and fired two shots, one in each thigh. He dropped to the floor with a thud. However, she didn't expect the beefy vamp behind him to jump so high, or so quick. Both shots missed him before the gun was knocked from her hand as she was knocked to the floor. It was then that Anthony ran for the back of the bar, but he was pulled back by the tattooed barman and threw across the room. He smashed straight through a wooden table at the other end of the room and found himself covered in a mixture of alcohol and his own blood.

Rose made a break for it the other way, but found herself face to face with Cerevad, that was the last thing she saw before he punched her square in the face knocking her unconscious. Anthony couldn't move. He was in shock, in the last thirty seconds he had learned that vampires existed and found himself locked in room with five of them. He found the courage to try and get up, but a foot on his chest stopped him from going anywhere.

CHAPTER 29

FACTORY SETTINGS

Helena, Rachel and Nicole (inside Margaret's body) suddenly found themselves in some sort of run-down warehouse or factory. None of them had a chance to take much in before they all passed out. Elathan didn't have enough energy to transport them all so had to use their energy to finish the job. It was nearly an hour before Holly even noticed them lying on the floor. It took her ages to get the trio upstairs and into beds to recover.

They all slept for two days straight leaving Holly frantically worrying about what had happened. Helena was the first to wake. The first thing that she noticed was the six beds that surrounded her, only two of them occupied. Helena guessed the shapes were Rachel and whatever her other sister was called at that time. Then she noticed someone else in the room, somebody sitting in a chair reading a book.

"He... ll ...o." Helena said through a series of yawns.

The woman put the book down. For a second Helena thought it was Margaret, then she noticed her hair wasn't ginger, it was purple. Her natural brown hair only visible at her roots.

"Morning." Holly said putting the book down and making her way over.

"Hi I'm Helena." She said before offering her hand.

Holly pushed it out of the way and went for the hug.

"So, that must be Margaret then." Holly confirmed looking over to one of the sleeping girls.

"Yeah, and you are?" Helena said pulling the blankets off her and getting up with a stretch.

Holly inspected Helena's face a little as if finding the similarities and differences before she answered.

"Holly. Who's that?" Holly said pointing over to the other woman.

"Rachel." She helped us escape the asylum.

Holly looked unconvinced.

"We couldn't have got out without her." Helena defended.

"If you say so." Holly said matter-of-factly

Helena noticed a strange smell was lingering in the air, she sniffed the asylum clothes she was still wearing and ashamedly realised she was the source. She decided a shower and a change of clothes were her first priority.

"Do you have any…?"

"Washing facilities yeah, showers are downstairs, far left corner."

Helena was ashamed but pleased she had the means to do something about it.

"Right well I'm gonna…"

Holly didn't acknowledge anything, she seemed more interested with who Rachel was. Helena decided to go get shower but she couldn't leave without confirming something first.

"Holly." Helena began.

"Yes."

"Are we..." Helena was still unsure how to ask even though she had started her question.

"Sisters?... Yes." Holly confirmed with a smile.

"Right. Good." Helena simply said before scuttling off to get cleaned up.

Once downstairs, Helena entered the shower cubicles apprehensively. The walls were dirty white, the floor was covered in cracked blue lino, and the ceiling looked grey with patches of damp. Helena looked into the shower bay, five showerheads stood idle against the wall. On a nearby bench sat three sets of clothes and towel combinations, as if Holly had anticipated their first move. Helena grabbed a towel placing it within grasp of the bays. She walked into the shower bay before taking off her clothes and discarding them as far as she could throw them.

Helena turned on the first showerhead by its button, water ineffectively spurted out. It was more of a tap than a shower. She moved along to the next one as the cold air began to nip at her naked skin. Helena tried the second shower; this time the flow rate was more than acceptable. She stepped under it and began washing her face and blonde hair in the lukewarm water. The water had a musty smell to it but she didn't care. The uneven floor caused the trickling water to puddle around her feet. She looked down at the dark water appalled, offended by its colour.

While she was showering Helena thought about the last few days. She knew it had been rough, but never realised she would be so dirty. She spun round to wash her back and looked around the room before screaming in shock. She noticed Rachel was standing there looking at her. Helena instinctively covered her body as best she could, but was surprised to feel the warming sensation that came with Rachel's watching.

"Hiya. Mind if I join you?" Rachel asked while freely admiring what she could of Helena's naked body.

Helena didn't know what to say, or do. She was not the type of person that would normally share a shower. She had never done it with her husband, never mind another woman. However, something about the situation felt normal, and she felt an unusual confidence about her own body that she had never felt before, but embarrassment got the better of her.

"I'm done now anyway." Helena decided, running out of the shower bay covering her modesty.

"Fair enough. Maybe some other time." Rachel said before taking her top off to reveal her bra. Helena didn't reply, but she could not resist glancing back at Rachel as she grabbed her clothes and headed for the nearest changing room. Once the door was closed she stood there confused. She was normally a strong-willed, mature and a feisty woman, but something about this situation made her feel like a silly teenager again. She felt awkward yet excited at the same time. She dismissed her thoughts to concentrate on getting dried and ready. Once ready she began to feel normal again, clean and complete.

Helena quickly left the shower area and followed the noise of conversation until she found Holly and her other sister in one of the factory's many side rooms. The confident stance showed Nicole was in control of the body this time. The room was previously an office, complete with an array of chairs that sat opposite a giant whiteboard. Wrote on the board with a thick black ink was six names. Holly, Helena, Margaret/Nicole, Alyson, Melissa. Four of the names were circled, leaving just Alyson and Melissa. It was obvious what it meant.

"There's two more of us then?" Helena announced her presence in the room.

"Yeah, but that's only the start of the fun." Nicole announced.

"Okay, so what's the plan? Like the overall master plan?" Helena asked. She didn't want all the little details, she wasn't even sure if she could accept everything that had happened so far.

"Top and bottom of it, Mam was betrayed by a daemon and is now a slave in Hell, we need to get her out. We need all six sisters and a shit-load of stuff to do it." Holly bluntly confirmed.

"Can't Elathan just do that thing he does?" Helena asked. She knew he couldn't, life wasn't that simple anymore. "...speaking of which, where is he?"

"Pulled back to Hell, he won't be visiting for a while after using the energy he used getting you four here. And getting out of Hell is impossible without a portal." Holly informed.

"So how do we open a Portal?" Helena asked.

Holly ignored her and walked over to the corner of the room. Cheap mismatched shelves were filled with numerous books. Some looked brand new, others looked centuries old. They were all magick books. Holly picked up one of the bigger books. She carried it to the table in the centre of the room and dropped it. The weight of the book dispersed dust throughout the room causing Helena and Nicole to cough. Holly waited for the air to clear before clearing the excess dust from its front leather sleeve. It read;

Magick – Darkest Spells

CHAPTER 30

SURVIVAL

Anthony tried to get up again but found himself pinned to the wooden floor. He looked up so see the man they had followed here looking down at him.

"Who are you?" Cerevad asked. His question seemed more genuine than threatening.

"Have you got David?" Anthony asked. He didn't know where his newly found bravery had come from, but he wasn't scared, just angry.

"Ah I get it, you're David Sixsmith's friends."

Cerevad released his foot from Anthony's chest while laughing. He went back to his borrowed pint and took a large gulp.

"Ahhhhh." Cerevad sounded upon swallowing the refreshment. He proceeded to lick his lips savouring the taste as he returned to Anthony.

"Now. What's the best way to consume you I wonder?" He kneeled down for a closer look at him.

It was then that Anthony saw Rose getting up from the floor across the room, the other vamps hadn't noticed her. She managed to pick up a chair before any of them even sensed her presence. She smashed it over the biggest of the four vamps, who immediately fell to the floor. The chair had smashed into a dozen pieces leaving Rose defenceless. She swung a punch at the vampire closest to her, the gangly looking one. He anticipated her attack and managed to catch her fist before squeezing it. Rose felt and heard her knuckles crack under his strength. The commotion had distracted Cerevad enough for Anthony to aim a boot straight into his crotch. Cerevad went down like a sack of potatoes, howling like a werewolf.

"Kill 'em" He squeaked in anger from the floor.

Despite being in immense pain Rose managed to get her knee up and into the gangly vamp's side before booting him away from her. She lunged for him as he fell to the floor, but the vamp managed to kick her feet away before she arrived. She fell to the floor with a thud and was quickly pinned on her front by the vamp who she had shot earlier. He seemed unaffected considering he had a bullet in each leg. He was so strong that Rose couldn't move from her front.

Anthony ran to help her but the tattooed barman grabbed him by the throat, he grinned a wide grin as Anthony dangled in mid-air. Rose and Anthony both squirmed hopelessly, Anthony felt his life ebbing away as he struggled for air. The room began to fade. Anthony could do nothing but watch as the gangly vamp moved in towards Rose's neck with his fangs on show. He was about to take a bite when the sound of a door being kicked stopped him in his tracks.

Cerevad propped himself up as the door was kicked in. Three people walked in with guns pointed. While they glanced around the room Cerevad took a deep sniff, two vamps and a human.

"You're the back-up I presume. Bit late don't you think." Cerevad sneered.

"Put them down." The biggest of the three demanded. He was built like a bull.

Anthony took a deep breath as the grip around his throat loosened. The four vamps suddenly seemed uninterested in their human prey and turned their attention to the newcomers allowing Rose to crawl across the floor to Anthony. As Anthony caught his breath Rose looked up to see Cerevad making a quick exit through the front door.

"Come on quick." Rose said helping Anthony up.

The pair of them didn't look back as the shouting, smashing and gunfire occurred behind them. They made it outside and were half-way up the street before a voice yelled at them.

"You two, wait!"

Rose turned to see it was the bulky one from the trio that turned up with the guns.

"Please let us go. We have to get to a hospital." Rose lied.

One of the other men came out and whispered something to the bulky man, he seemed to pause and think for a moment. Rose stood waiting, hoping.

"Can you get to the hospital yourself?" The man asked.

"Yes." Rose replied quickly.

"Very well. Goodbye and good luck." The man confirmed.

Rose breathed a sigh of relief, she couldn't help it. She smiled and turned her back on the man as she helped Anthony towards the car.

"One more thing..." The man shouted back causing Rose to stop dead in her tracks.

She glanced around looking for anything that could help her, anything she could use as a weapon. A severed piece of brick was the only thing Rose spotted. She loosened her grip on Anthony, ready to dive for it.

"...were you bitten by any of them?" The bulky man finalised.

"No." Rose exclaimed with relief. "Neither of us were." She added.

"Very well. Good day." The man shouted before disappearing back inside Priveam.

Rose ignored him and kept walking, desperate to get away before he changed his mind. As she arrived at her car with her arm around Anthony, she knew they had been lucky to escape. Problem was, the man with the briefcase (who turned out to be a vampire named Cerevad) had also escaped.

Meanwhile Torus, Trigger and Ryan were busy cleaning up the mess they had caused in Priveam. It was then that they found Celeste, the owner of the bar, tied up in the back room. She was a little beaten-up, but alive. She went on to tell them that the four dead vampires on the floor were responsible for tying her up, but one of them was missing and that the two humans they had just let go had nothing to do with it.

CHAPTER 31

MISSING FRIENDS

David rushed into the hallway. Winwood, Chora and Legitus had returned from their investigation. There was still no sign of the other group. David thought it was an ideal opportunity to ask if there was any chance he could see his friend Anthony. More than anything he just wanted to share all of his recent experiences with someone that would understand the gravitas of the situation. He walked up to Winwood and blurted out the question without really thinking it through.

"Will I ever get to see any of my friends or family?" David asked.

Winwood stopped in his tracks pondering the best way to answer. The rest of the group pretended to look like they weren't eavesdropping and disappeared in all directions. They didn't do a very good job, David could sense they were listening around each corner.

"In my life, I have watched my parents die, then my siblings and friends and then my children. Since then, I have lost my grandchildren, then my grandchildren's children and their children after that."

"I'm sorry to hear that." David sympathised. He didn't realise how selfish it was to ask until that moment.

"Look I know you miss certain people in your life. Unfortunately, it is the way of the vampire world. Humans aren't supposed to know about us, it's too dangerous for the both of us." Winwood informed.

"But Maude and Ryan know about us. Surely there are other humans who can help too." David reasoned.

"Some are aware of our existence, yes. But those people weren't told. They learnt about us of their own accord, and are now vowed to a life of secrecy. A life of lies, a life of danger. They choose that risk when they become involved in the vampire world. We cannot choose to put new people in that situation, especially for the benefit of ourselves." Winwood countered.

There was a pause while David tried to think of a loophole in the system, a way he could get what he wanted, but deep down he knew he was fighting a losing battle. He knew it was wrong of him to pursue this anymore and eventually he conceded defeat with a single word.

"Sorry." David gave in.

"Don't worry, it's only natural to wanna share a new experience with someone familiar. However, I hope you understand why we cannot?" Winwood sympathised as they walked the corridor.

"I do thanks." David sulked as they arrived at Winwood's office.

"And anyway, I'm hoping you find yourself among new friends with us?" Winwood said with a wink as he opened his office door. David appreciated the effort, but he knew nobody could replace the hole of not having your best friend with you, especially when you're on an adventure.

"Get some sleep for now, you'll need it. I need you and Paige field ready asap." Winwood announced as he closed his office door.

David walked back to his room feeling confused. He had never felt excited and dejected at the same time before.

Meanwhile, Winwood was sat looking through some notes when his mobile phone began to ring. He looked at the dialler, it was Torus.

"Hello." He started.

"Hi Boss. Sorry for the delay, we hit a snag." Torus informed.

"What happened?" Winwood urged.

"We ran into a little trouble at Priveam. We had to put four vamps down. One got away. I think it was Cerevad, but I didn't get a proper look."

"I'm sure you did what you had to do. How's Celeste?"

"She's okay, a little beaten-up, but you know what she's like. Real tough cookie."

"You best bring her to the base, tell her I said she has to come." Winwood suggested.

"Will do. Oh, and I don't know if it was anything, but there were two humans here before, I let them go, they weren't bitten or anything. Think they were just in the wrong place, at the wrong time." Torus updated.

"We'll have to watch them in case Cerevad is up to his old tricks again. But for now, just get back to the base." Winwood ordered before hanging up,

CHAPTER 32

THE LIFE OF HOLLY HAMILTON

Holly Hamilton was an ordinary twenty-seven-year-old with an unusual sense of style. She had dyed purple hair and wore gothic style jewellery and clothing; it was a phase that stuck. She worked a normal job and lived in an average flat. Her upbringing wasn't usual, nor was it unheard of. Her foster parents cared, but cared enough to let her make her own mistakes, and there was plenty, more than they knew. She respected them for it and never even thought about her real family, not until her best friend died of a brain tumour and she realised her own mortality. She thought it couldn't hurt to try and track down her real Mam and Dad, and to find out if she had any siblings.

At the start, all she had was the name of her mother, Emily Bailey. Holly went through numerous adoptive agencies and family tree websites before finally uncovering a death certificate dated shortly after Holly's birth. Holly didn't shed a tear, but it did bother her. The feeling of loss stayed with her for weeks until she made a decision. She would visit her mother's grave, forget this whole business, and go back to her normal life.

Several weeks later, she set off on a train to Edinburgh armed with a suitcase and a week off work. She left her bags at the hotel and went straight to the cemetery. Holly arrived to a sea of fog, and the smell of newly-mowed wet grass. The process of reading every single gravestone would have been a boring one if it wasn't for Linkin Park playing through her earphones. Her heart skipped as she eventually found the reason she came. The epitaph on the gravestone read.

'Here lies the body

Of Emily Bailey.

Mother of 6 girls,

Died suddenly.

Aged 27 in 1990.

Rest in Peace.'

Holly removed her earphones in shock; they swung around her collar as she re-read the tombstone several times. As she eventually took it all in she fell, knees to the floor, sobbing her eyes out for a good few minutes. When she finally stopped crying, the only audible noise was the riff of guitars, the bang of drums and the screaming of indistinct lyrics swinging like a pendulum around her neck. She ripped the jack from its hole and wiped away the tears. She read the words once more.

"That means I've got five sisters." She realised aloud. She couldn't help the smile that lit up her face.

It was then that she noticed the small red box placed in front of the gravestone with a dying flower propped up from a hole in the lid. Holly picked it up to inspect it. It had gilded ribbons around it and felt wooden. Upon noticing a small clasp on the front, she opened it. Inside was a small key neatly packed inside some tissue paper. She took it out to inspect it with air of intrigue. Holly noticed a locker key number and a company name carved onto the exterior of the key. She looked around the cemetery half-expecting someone to be watching, waiting in the fog, but she couldn't see a soul. She took the key from the box and headed out of the cemetery with a vague sense of optimism.

After an hour of miss-matched directions she found herself at a cafe opposite Harpers. She had been told it was part bank, part storage company. After a bite to eat and a pot of tea Holly headed inside excitedly. The interior had a backdrop of blue coloured glass supported by white painted beams and columns. Nearly everything inside was a shade of orange or grey, including the people. She was soon directed to the inside of a small vault with numerous metal lockers.

"This is one of our oldest bids, over twenty years this has been here unopened." A man informed before keenly watching her fumble with the key. They were both surprised to see the contents. It was just a book, and not even a nice one, just a scraggy looking exercise book. The man looked devastated as he escorted her from the premises. Holly headed back to the cafe with the book clasped in hand. Equipped with a nice warm cup of cocoa topped with cream and chocolate sprinkles, she looked properly at the book. Upon inspection, the front and back cover were completely blank. Holly opened the front cover to reveal a page with a little black box. It read;

'Emily Bailey's Diary.'

Holly took a deep breath and thought for a moment. She knew she could not go back once she had started reading it. She pondered and took a sip of her cocoa. It warmed her through, but did little to distract her from the diary. Temptation quickly won her over and she began reading. It started with Emily at school, Pennywell Comprehensive in Sunderland. She went through all the typical teenage troubles from boys, to acceptance, to identity. Holly loved the parts about Emily being a rebel and *'dolling off'* from school. As her school days drew to a close so did her amount of entries.

By this point, Holly was so entranced in the diary's pages that her drink had gone cold and she had to order a new one. The book followed Emily's journey through college and then to the world of work at somewhere called Joplings. It told of the relationships, the good, and bad that she'd had. Eventually she settled with a mysterious man named Pete. He was a bit absent, but they seemed happy enough. Holly then arrived at a page with only one entry, just three words filled the paper.

"I am pregnant."

She quickly turned over but the following page was blank, and the next, and the next. Holly frustratingly began turning pages until she arrived at the back of the book. There was no more text, just a telephone number in the back. Holly downed her lukewarm cocoa and smiled with excitement as she left the café. She carefully copied the number from the book into her mobile phone and pressed the green button. It rang a few times before it was answered.

"Hello." Answered the croaky voice of an old woman.

"Hi. I found this number in a diary I was just wondering who it is?" Holly started.

"Nine Primrose Hill." The old woman replied before hanging up.

Holly didn't know what to do or say next. She was excited yet disappointed. Part of her wished it was her Dad that had answered the phone.

CHAPTER 33

THE LIFE OF HOLLY HAMILTON

PART 2

Holly paid the taxi driver and looked up at her location. She was surprised to find the address was a business and not the home address that she expected to find. The building was a glass fronted shop fronted with an old looking red and white sign that read 'Mitchell and Mitchell.' Holly took a deep breath before finally entering. She didn't know what to expect as she approached the shop, but presumed it would be a similarly long-winded journey as her last leg.

A bell chimed above as she squeezed open the door. Holly looked around for a counter and eventually located it through the maze of goods the store had to offer. It was packed from floor to ceiling with dusty chandeliers, rusty railway signs and half broken furniture. She wormed her way through everything to an old woman who was sat reading a magazine. She glanced up as Holly got closer and then continued reading.

"Hi, I think I might have spoken to you earlier." Holly started.

The woman got up ignoring her; she headed straight for the entrance. Holly was about to say something until the old woman turned the sign on the front door to say 'Shop Closed.' and headed back towards her.

"I didn't think it would take this long for one of you to come." The old woman said as she passed Holly and went behind the counter. She indicated Holly to follow her into the back of the store.

Holly obliged and found herself in a more colourful and organised room. It was a minimalist part kitchen, part library. The walls shone an orange backdrop.

"Drink?" The old woman asked heading towards one of the three kettles that sat on display.

"No thanks."

Holly glanced at a couple of books on the shelves. They were all about fantasy and magick. Holly smiled at the old woman as she returned with two cups of grey looking tea. The woman had big bushy grey hair and looked rather frail. If Holly were to guess she would have gone with 'eighties'. Holly took the tea, putting it down on a nearby coaster as the woman got settled in an armchair. It was silent for a while; Holly was forced to start.

"What did you mean when you said you didn't think it would take so long for one of us to come?"

"Well if you have the diary, you must have seen the gravestone right?" The woman replied with a grin before sipping her tea.

"You mean me and my five sisters?" Holly asked.

"Yes and no." The old woman informed.

"What do you mean yes and no?"

"Your mother gave birth to six, but one of your sisters' bodies wasn't strong enough. We were forced to make two of you share the same body, you must understand it was the only way." The old woman pleaded as if she expected to be punished. Holly tried to take in the information, but she was already planning her next question.

"What do you mean share a body? And who's we?" Holly demanded.

"Me and another witch called Lucille. There's two minds in one body, I suppose it's like what people call split personality. It's not natural, but it was the only way."

Holly took a deep breath in an attempt to calm down, she found herself getting angry and wanting to shout. She took a sip of tea, it was deliciously cold, far too much milk.

"How did you know my mother?" Holly asked after a while

"We used to perform magick together?" The woman replied before finishing her tea.

"Like Paul Daniels, illusions and stuff?"

"No. I mean real magick, none of this rubber knives, hats and rabbits shit." The woman said getting up from her seat. Holly went to help her up, but she was up so quick she didn't have a chance.

"What's real magick?" Holly asked before taking the leap and downing the cold cup of tea. She nearly choked on the sugar cube at the bottom. The old woman didn't notice, she was so busy rifling through shelves of books as if looking for one in particular. She hovered over one for a moment before pulling it from the shelf. She carried it over and gave it to Holly who now looked confused.

The book was called Daemonology - Contacting and Summoning. Holly knew a little about daemons from the movies and television she watched, but the book somehow felt more genuine than them. Holly looked back up at the woman, she looked another year older every time Holly looked at her.

"What am I supposed to do with this?"

"Summon a daemon called Elathan. He will tell you everything you need to know. Now go, before you bring any unwanted attention." The old woman finalised as she went into a coughing fit. Holly wanted to make sure she was okay but was quickly ushered out of the shop and into the street. She was beginning to feel like this whole journey had been for nothing or was some sort of prank. All she had to show for her time was a stupid book and her mother's diary.

*****

Three months later Holly's life had gone through some significant changes. She had been made redundant from her job, lost her flat, and some of her friends in the process. Holly was back living with her adoptive parents and rummaging through things to sell when she came across the Daemonology book she was given by the elderly woman. She had yet to turn a page in it, and decided to have a glance through. The frontispiece contained no words, just an upside-down star with numerous symbols placed haphazardly around it. As Holly turned the page her heart skipped a beat. Inked on the inside of a printed box were the words;

'This book belongs to Emily Bailey'

Holly smiled upon noticing the similarity in her mother's writing style with her own, something she hadn't even picked up when she read through the diary. She touched the words on the page with a delicacy as if they held some sort of connection to her mother. She thought for a moment to try and picture her face but nothing would quite come to mind. It was the first time she longed to see her real mother, and father for that matter. Holly dismissed her efforts and turned the next page. It was a contents page, it read;

Holly read down the list, it sounded interesting but she wasn't in the mood for in-depth reading, she skipped straight to Section 5: Basic magick spells. The spells were divided into opposite sections. Love and un-love spells, curses and reverse curses, good luck and bad luck. Holly flicked through until she arrived at Wealth/Money spells. She read aloud from the first box.

'Virii Peduniac'

She read on...

'This spell will increase the chances of obtaining extra wealth. IT WILL NOT give you physical money. Ingredients Needed...

Holly smiled upon reading the words.

1 Green Bowl, 4 Green Candles, A square piece of paper just larger than the bowl, 1 Dice, 1 Malachite Stone (The bigger the stone, the more effective the spell will be) and spring water.'

Holly continued to read on like a child at Christmas.

''Money, money, please be mine.

Bring me this and I'll be fine.

I'm harming no-one, it's for me.

Money, money, set me free.''

Holly almost laughed at the simplicity of it all. It sounded like some sort of children's magick book. Her bank balance of £1.13 and her intrigue spurred her on. She read the instructions.

1. Fill the bowl with water, place the paper inside the bowl, the middle of the paper should be underwater and outsides of the paper should be outside of the bowl.

2. Place the Malachite stone and dice on top of the paper. Place the four green candles around the bowl with equal distance apart.

3. Light the four candles and touch the malachite stone with your index finger and begin repeating the chant over and over, until the four candles have burnt out. The smell of heated paper should be in the air.

She laughed as she read the final words in bold at the bottom of the page. It was as if they dismissed every word she had read previous.

"PLEASE NOTE THAT YOU WILL NOT RECEIVE MONEY UNTIL YOU MAKE MORE OF AN EFFORT TO SEEK MONEY!"

Holly closed the book and dismissed the whole idea, for days. It was only when she got sick of asking to borrow money that she went back to the book. She gathered all the ingredients and on a rain soaked Thursday she finally began the spell. Holly carefully put everything in place, lit the candles, took a deep breath then began the chant. She repeated it with genuine hope until the candles finally burnt out. Holly inhaled a deep breath to smell the air. The lingering scent of the candles was all she could get from the aroma. It was supposed to smell of heated paper.

Holly got up angrily but she almost fell to the floor as she stood. She felt really light-headed and nauseous all of a sudden. It was as if the spell had taken some of her energy, the feeling gave her hope that it might yet have actually worked. She eventually managed to stand without assistance and left her parents' house in search of money. Within an hour, she managed to find a tenner and secure a job interview. It was only when she got her first payslip two weeks later, that it occurred to her she might be able to perform magick.

CHAPTER 34

FIRST MISSION

David was awoken early by Torus, and he quickly found himself tiredly stretching in the training room. His fight training began with the same attacks and blocks he had learnt previously, but this time he had to be stronger and faster. In no time at all he had gone from a cowardly human forced to walk the wrong way to college, to a vampire ready for a fight.

After a McDonalds breakfast brought in by Doc and Ryan, they all had a bunch of sparring sessions. David couldn't beat his sparring partners Ryan or Paige yet, but he gave it a good go and managed to land a couple of decent blows, even if he did feel guilty about it after. But learning to take a blow was just as important as learning to hit someone, Doc explained to David as he nurses David's injuries with an ice pack.

"Taking a hit without losing your temper is a really good sign." Doc reminded as he and David watched the rest of the group sparring, trying to learn a thing or two from each of the fights. Ryan was quite tough for a human and easily outmatched Paige and Trigger. But he couldn't best Chora or Legitus, who were both pretty evenly matched. Torus, however, was a league above everyone else.

The afternoon's session was filled with pins, grappling, throws and breakfalls. David found himself practicing with Trigger, who was told off twice for being too gentle with David. The throws and falls didn't particularly hurt but David was grateful when the session

161

come to an end. Everything felt bruised and he felt like he was on the verge of keeling over when they finally did stop for some tea.

Doc had prepared them all an impressive Sunday Lunch. There was broccoli, carrots, turnip, mash, sausages, Yorkshire puddings, roast potatoes and stuffing balls, all smothered in a red wine and squirrel blood gravy. It was lovely. After the bait, David retreated back to bed with a content belly and aching body.

The next morning David awoke with a groan; most of his body hurt and his limbs felt restrictive in movement. He drank a cup of blood before and after his shower. He was only half dried and ready when a knock at his door interrupted his momentum. He didn't have his top on yet but yelled "Come in." anyway. He was startled to see Chora enter the room and quickly did his best to cover up the top half of his body with his towel before she noticed how feeble and skinny he was. Chora noticed his drastic cover up and couldn't help but grin.

"Sorry, I can see you're busy, just came to tell you Winwood's back. We have a meeting in five." Chora announced.

"Okay thanks." David said quickly, desperate for her to leave the room.

"See you there." Chora added turning her back to David and walking outside.

David breathed a sigh of relief; he had always been slightly embarrassed about his body. He walked towards the door to close it.

"Nice pecs by the way." Chora shouted back from around the corner.

David was simple euphoric, he wasn't used to compliments, especially from women. He was excited by the prospect that he actually stood a chance with such a beautiful woman, even though she did shoot him the first time they met. He changed his mind and shook it off as banter before getting ready and leaving.

David made his way to the meeting room and was rather surprised to find almost everybody was already there waiting for him. He apologised for keeping them waiting and quickly sat down. It was then that he noticed somebody new in the room. It was a woman with jet black hair and a slim but strong looking physique; she was covered in tattoos and piercings.

"David this is Celeste. Celeste, David." Winwood indicated.

They both nodded an acknowledgment as Winwood continued speaking.

"For those wondering where Legitus and Ryan are, I have sent them to find a couple of humans that were involved in an incident at a bar Celeste owns. I wanna know if they are somehow involved, or were just in the wrong place at the wrong time. Also, we have a lot on at the minute so we will have to put a hold on the training and send everybody on missions."

Although David enjoyed the martial arts lesson the day before he couldn't be happier he was getting a break from it, it was a painful lesson to say the least.

"So, what's happening?" Doc queried, he too was keen to get out of the base for a change.

"Well as you know Priveam was took over by a gang of vamps yesterday. Celeste was lucky you guys turned up out the blue." Winwood informed.

"Yeah thanks guys." Celeste interjected.

"No worries." Torus put forward on behalf of the group.

"Now we have to find out who these vamps were, and why they took over Priveam in the first place. Were they just rogue's, or did they have a purpose, how long have they been in the area, so on, so forth. So Doc, you'll be pleased to know you're getting out of the base for this one."

"Thank God." Doc joked.

"And you'll be pleased to know you and Celeste are having a night out. I want you going around other bars asking questions. I'm not bothered about minor law breaking or infringements, just stick to the mission on this one, there's too much time and paperwork involved for anything else. Just go for a few drinks, rustle a few feathers, see what's what?"

"Fine by me." Doc excitedly finalised.

"Now next job, I've heard from a source this morning that something happened in Ludlow yesterday that has made the local news. Apparently three women have 'literally disappeared' from a psychiatric hospital." Winwood informed.

"Is this related to Helena?" Chora asked.

"I'm not sure, but that's what you and David are going to find out. You can take the jeep." Winwood announced.

David was forced to bite his top lip to hide his grin. He was positively beaming to be working with Chora, especially alone.

"You will be meeting a man called Mr Jewson tomorrow morning, who has agreed to answer some questions on the events last night. Just find out if it's a normal escape, or if they got out by supernatural means, and see if it has any similarities with the disappearance of Helena Pearce."

"Okay." Chora confirmed with a smile towards David. David smiled back with far too much glee.

"Now Trigs and Torus, Tom Pearce hasn't seen you guys yet, I want you to follow him for a few days to see if we can rule him out of our Helena investigation." Winwood said before handing over a piece of paper with his location and a bank card to check-in to the hotel with.

"Okay no problem." Torus said taking them.

"As for me and Paige, we have a meeting with the VRG."

Everyone looked shocked and slightly jealous of this revelation.

"What's the VRG?" David quietly asked Doc.

"Vampire Royal Guard." Doc whispered back.

"I have no idea what its regarding, but I will let you know, as soon as we know. Please be careful and don't do anything I wouldn't." Winwood announced.

Everyone left them room armed with their orders and partners, keen to crack on with their individual missions. David followed Chora to the jeep like a lapdog and was excited to spend time with her, but they struggled for conversation for most of the journey. Their awkward journey there lasted two hours and David was disappointed to find himself staying the night in a sub-standard safe house. Although he wouldn't admit it, the place creeped him out. With nothing to do until the next day they sat in silence for a while before David got up to head to bed.

"Where you going?" Chora asked as he headed towards the stairs.

"I was gonna head to bed. What else is there to do here?" David sulkily responded.

"You could have a drink with me." Chora suggested with a smile before getting up and heading to an overnight bag she had brought with her.

"Okay." David answered turning around to see her remove two bottles from her bag. One was red, the other white.

"I hope you don't mind I stole them from your party. It's rare we get to drink." Chora said with a grin putting the two bottles down and heading into the kitchen in search of some glasses.

"Not at all." David said with a shy giggle.

She returned empty handed. It didn't kill her optimism and she quickly opened the red bottle taking a large swig before offering it to David. He took a swig and almost choked, it was stronger than he expected it to be. It tasted like wine but had the kick of whisky. They both burst into a fit of laughter as he wiped the excess booze he had spilt from around his mouth.

CHAPTER 35

ONE STEP BACK

Anthony and Rose got into the car awkwardly, their injuries reminding them of their recent fight for survival. As Rose drove off neither of them said a word, and it stayed like that a good thirty-minutes until Rose eventually pulled over into a housing estate. Rose pulled out her phone from her inside pocket. She didn't look surprised to see the screen had been smashed. As she unlocked it she was grateful to realise it still worked.

"Hi Rose." An ecstatic and surprised voice yelled through the phone.

"Sarah, I need your help." Rose commanded. There was a seriousness in her voice. The same one Anthony recognised from when he first met Rose back at the police station. It was just a few weeks ago, but it felt like months.

"What's it this time?" Sarah asked unfazed.

"I'm coming to yours. I need a doctor, someone who knows what they're doing."

"For you?"

"Not just me."

There was a silence over the phone.

"What you got yourself into now?" The voice asked but Rose didn't reply.   "...Fine, I will see what I can do. You owe me this time though, you're out of favours."

"Thanks Sarah."

Rose didn't give her a chance to say goodbye before she hung up the phone.

Rose peeled her hand from the steering wheel and tried to straighten her fingers out, she couldn't. Anthony noticed her hand had now gone a dark shade of purple, he'd never seen a bruise so dark, or one appear so quickly.

"Make sure we aren't being followed. I don't want any surprises when we get to where we are going." Rose demanded before starting up the car again.

She drove slower this time as if her injuries were finally taking their toll. Anthony didn't pay any attention to where they were going and he soon found himself in unfamiliar territory.

"Well?" Rose asked as they pulled up next to a series of four garage doors. One of them was already open.

"I don't think so..." Anthony said worryingly. He wasn't used to this sort of work and wasn't really sure what he was doing. "Nothing has..." He began, but then he felt a dizziness spread over him, he watched the interior of the car spin around him and that was the last thing he saw before he passed out.

*****

Anthony woke up on a bed nearly two whole days later. He tried to sit up, but the pain in his chest stopped him. He removed the blankets covering his torso to reveal a mass of bandages wrapped around him like he was some sort of mummy. He looked around the room for a clue to where he was. A white dresser full of make-up in the corner of the room revealed it was possibly an adult woman's room. He noticed the smell of tomato soup before he heard the footsteps that were bringing it, it was Rose. Anthony sat up as best he could to receive and balance the lap-tray that she brought him. She too was injured, she had a cast on her right wrist, or something that at least resembled a cast.

"How you doing?" Rose asked while carefully handing over the lap tray.

"Been better, you?" Anthony asked before having a look at the goods she had brought him. There was a yellow bowl full of tomato soup, half a baguette, and a dollop of butter. A posh looking spoon, a small glass a water and some painkillers made up the rest of the tray.

"I'll live. My friend thinks you've bruised all your ribs and pulled a bunch of your muscles, hence the bandages. She wants to monitor you today and tomorrow just in case."

"Thanks, how's your hand?" Anthony questioned before shifting his weight to get himself comfortable and ready to eat.

"Painful." Rose joked. "I have a bunch of small but clean fractures." Rose said inspecting her cast. "I will leave you to eat. I will be back in a bit." She said as she noticed Anthony was looking rather keen to eat. He couldn't remember the last time he was this hungry. Anthony was pleased as she disappeared; he loved her company but he didn't like eating in front of people, even if it was just soup.

When Rose returned later on. Anthony was fed and watered. She sat silently on the edge of the bed for a while clearly not wanting to start the conversation.

"So, what now?" Anthony asked half-expecting to find out their search for David and Daisy would end now.

"I've got a new lead..." Rose started. Her face told Anthony that wasn't all she had to say.

"But..." Anthony urged.

"But my friend said you shouldn't move for a few days." She sympathised.

"Okay so I'm done, is that what you're saying?" Anthony shouted back.

"God no..." Rose said before pausing to think her words through carefully, she put her hand on his leg. "...You're not getting out of this fight that easily. You're just sitting this round out that's all..."

Anthony had to stop himself from crying. He knew they were together in this through thick and thin, and they would continue the road they started wherever or whoever, it led to next.

"...Besides it's just a boring meeting with some bloke up Scotland. I'll be back to take you home tomorrow." Rose sympathised.

"Thanks Rose." Anthony said sincerely. He hadn't known Rose very long and she had already done so much for him, including saving his life.

"No, thank you. I'm closer to finding out what happened to Daisy than I've ever been thanks to you." Rose got up and walked to a nearby ottoman, she grabbed a phone and gave it to Anthony.

"I will be in touch, just get yourself rested." Rose said before grabbing his lap tray and heading towards the door.

"I will do thanks."

"Oh, and you might want to ring your mam and tell her you're okay." Rose said with a smile before leaving. Anthony looked down at his phone to reveal 79 missed calls and 54 texts, they were all from his mam and aunty.

He sniggered before ringing her straight away.

CHAPTER 36

DARK MAGICK

After a hard day's slog Holly Hamilton returned home and went straight upstairs and into her magick book. She had a few magick spells under her belt now, but she had never looked through the book while she was angry. She didn't want her manager dead exactly, just to teach her a lesson. She began reading through the Curses, Hexes and Jinxes. She had normally skipped this part of the book, so what she did read was for the first time. A paragraph stood as a solitary warning before any spells were written. She read it aloud for fear of missing something.

This section of the book is full of spells that may cause irreversible damage to the person/person's they are inflicted against. The energy that a Wicca uses when casting such spells can also be addictive, and may therefore have unwanted side effects. Please be sure you want to proceed before doing so....

Holly laughed; she wasn't going to be put off by simple words of warning. If her manager was gone they would have no choice but to promote Holly. It was a necessary evil. She read on...

Bad Luck Spells, Breaking Up a Couple Spells, Friends Apart Spells, Money Liquidation Spells. Evil Eye Spell.

Holly stopped and looked at the page number for the evil eye spell and skipped across to it.

'Evil Eye Spell'

This spell will create havoc in the person's life it is cast against. It works by opening her karma to all negative residual energy and could cause anything from hiccups to death. '

Holly laughed at the thought of the hiccups, but the mention of death made her feel a little uneasy and guilty about it. Suddenly her mother flashed in her head, a clear image of her, brown hair, twenties, it was as if she was warning Holly not to do it. Then for some reason her thoughts skipped back to the old woman in the shop who had told her to call a daemon.

Holly flipped through the book and eventually found the page. 'Calling a daemon.' She looked at the page for a moment and touched it softly with her hand feeling the paper beneath her now sweaty palm. She longed to see her mother. As she moved across the page she noticed a word written in pencil in the top right-hand corner. It read ''Elathan''. She quickly read through the ingredients for fear she might change her mind at any point.

3 White Candles, A bowl with stagnant water, a knife. Some paint or something similar to draw the following seal on the floor. Holly looked at the seal, seemed easy enough. It was just a circle with a pentagram inside, with a number of sigils in each triangle around the outside, sigils that she didn't recognise. Holly quickly gathered all the ingredients and began spraying the floor without even thinking about staining the carpet.

As she began to follow the spell instructions she began to get excited, even if she was a little nervous. Twenty minutes later the candles were lit, the seal was haphazardly sprayed on the floor and she had the knife ready to cut her hand. She winced as she sliced the palm of her hand and bled into a bowl, the pain of the cut stemmed right through her hand. As she placed the blood-laden dish into the centre of the room everything was in place, she stood back and began the chant.

"Oh daemon, daemon, I call you forth.

Please hear my call ... Elathan.

Candles light your way to me,

Blood is my sacrifice to you,

Temporary freedom be your reward.

So, may you help me and find my seal, your ward."

Holly breathed quietly in anticipation, eyes at their peripheral, ears cocked. She felt the drowsy feeling rise over her again, the same feeling that came with most successful spells. She fearfully scanned the room. As her head moved back towards the seal she got the shock of her life as she noticed a man standing there. He looked like a smart businessman with his suit and tie, but his gruff demeanour was more animalistic in nature.

"How do you know my name woman?" He asked while instinctively looking around the room. He seemed to be paying particular attention to the floor and ceiling.

"It was written in a book." Holly answered nervously. Suddenly this wasn't such a good idea.

She watched him inspect the room. His main focus was on the floor and the ceiling.

"Only one seal. You're new to this." The man stated still looking around the room.

"Magick no. It is my first time calling a daemon though." Holly informed.

Holly felt dejected that the man thought she was an amateur; she was quite proud of the spells she had achieved so far.

Without warning the daemon stamped on the floor knocking the candles over, a single flame from one of them burnt quickly across the carpet and melted some of the paint creating a hole in the seal. The daemon escaped, zooming towards Holly with lightning speed, grabbing her by the throat. By the time she realised what was happening it was too late and she was pinned against a nearby wall.

"Why did you call me?" He asked before loosening his grip on her throat, just enough to let her talk.

"I was told to call you." Holly pleaded.

"By whom?" The man asked lowering her feet to the floor but keeping a tight grip of her throat.

"An old woman...she used to do magick with my mam...I don't know the woman's name."

The daemon let go of her. Holly endured a splurge of coughing while the man stood there deep in thought.

"You must be one of the six? I'm sorry, please forgive me." The man helped Holly up from the floor before stamping out the small fire he had created. He opened the window to let out the pillar of spoke and adjusted his suit before taking a seat on her unmade bed.

"Yes. I'm Holly, I take it your Elathan?" Holly asked when she finally found enough air in her lungs to breath.

"Yes, I'm Elathan. How many of them have you found?"

"How many what?"

"Of your sisters?" Elathan asked glancing at his watch.

"None."

"Well you will have to get a move on, your mothers waiting." Elathan got up glancing around the room. He studied random elements as if he was curious about human life.

"What do you mean waiting? She's dead... isn't she?"

"Everyone can die once. Your mother's in Hell, and we are going to get her out. But first you have to find your sisters to do the spell." The daemon said slowly to make sure Holly understood.

"What spell?" Holly asked.

He looked down at his watch again. Holly got the feeling she was on a schedule.

"Call me in a week and I'll explain more then, just the blood and the chant should be enough next time." The daemon said before adjusting his suit. He looked like he was about to go into a meeting.

"Can I see her before...?" Holly began but it was too late, the daemon had already disappeared.

CHAPTER 37

BEGINNERS MAGICK

Holly finished explaining her life story to her sisters and Rachel. Talking through it all felt like she had unburdened herself, and bonded with her siblings at the same time. She felt normal for a change, like a normal family catching up over coffee. Everyone was quiet for a while afterwards, as if it was hard to take in everything that Holly had told them. Helena was the first to break the silence, and she went straight for the elephant in the room.

"So how do we do it, how do we get mum out of Hell?"

"There is a spell. It's called the six souls." Holly replied wishing she could have revelled in the normalness for just a few more seconds.

"And we need the other sisters for that?" Nicole asked.

"Yes." Holly replied.

"Can I help?" Rachel asked, feeling a little left out.

There was a pause as Holly looked at Helena, Holly didn't want anyone involved that didn't have to be, but Helena's glare forced her answer.

"We could do with all the help we could get, but you can't help with the final spell, it has to be just us, all the sisters." Holly obliged.

"Who is first?" Nicole asked.

"Alyson is closer, but I'd rather go for Melissa first. But, we are nowhere near ready for either of them yet to be honest." Holly informed.

"What do you mean?" Helena asked slightly offended.

"No offense but you's were the easy part. I've been doing magick for months now. Melissa has been at it for years. As for Alyson, let's just say she's in a league of her own."

The group stood in deflated silence while Holly walked over to the other side of the room and started going through a bunch of books, she eventually picked out three. She returned giving one to Helena, one to Nicole and one to Rachel while speaking.

"These are basic magick books. They will tell you everything you need to know about magick. Once I'm happy you can all defend yourselves, we can go after Melissa."

*****

The three girls spent the rest of the day reading from their respective spell books, but nobody actually attempted a spell, which Holly was glad about. Helena was fascinated to learn that the five elements of Fire, Water, Air, Earth and Lightning made up the five triangles within a pentagram. Hence, the reason for its famous iconography associated with witches, and that mastering the pentagram was your basic level one of being a witch.

The next day Holly allowed them to start practicing some basic magick spells. At first it was full rituals with incantations and a bunch of ingredients (which Holly had stacks of stored at the abandoned factory). However, the more they practiced a particular spell the less they needed to do it. They reduced the amount of ingredients they needed to do a spell until they no longer needed them. Eventually, even the incantation was made redundant and they could cast basic magick spells just by thinking of them.

Over the next few days the girls magick abilities branched off in different directions as each of them learned about their own particular interests. Margaret and Nicole (who were nicely taking turns with the body that they shared) chose to learn about fire and all the different things they could do with it. Rachel concentrated on water based spells, while Helena tried to mix her abilities up, she learnt a few different spells from each element.

By the end of the week the girls were practicing mini-duels against each other. Margaret and Nicole took turns training with Holly, while Helena teamed up with Rachel. Helena quickly developed a bit of a bond with Rachel, she wasn't sure if it was just a friendship or whether there was something else there. All she knew was, the more time she spent with Rachel, the more time she wanted to spend with Rachel.

CHAPTER 38

CHORA'S STORY

Chora and David attempted to get comfy in the middle of the hardwood floor because the furniture looked too dusty to sit on. He tried to get as close to her as he dared, without making it obvious. As they sat there silently drinking he longed for an accident brush of her skin, a closeness he had never experienced before. David had never been as attracted to someone as he was to Chora in that very moment. Even though she shot him recently.

"So how you finding your new life?' Chora asked taking another swig of the bottle and offering it back to David.

"It's brilliant but..." David sipped some contents and returned the bottle.

"...But you miss your old life right?" Chora said with a smile. She swigged and gave it back.

"That obvious?" David laughed.

"Most people do to be honest." Chora noted.

"It's not so much my life I miss, it was pretty awful to be honest, more so the people in it. What about you?"

"I had an easy life. I was part of a rich family called the Chesterfields. Catherine was my original name." Chora said while remembering her previous life. David was surprised, he had become so accustomed to calling her Chora he didn't think about what her previous name might have been. He began to wonder what the rest of the Libra vamps were originally called.

"What did you do, in your previous life I mean?" David queried in between another swig of booze. The more he drank the less awful it tasted.

"Well nothing really, my husband John earned all the money, and in them days the women of the house didn't do much. Most of my time was spent choosing fabrics, going for long walks and telling the servants what to do."

David rode the wave of jealousy the mention of marriage forced. He was also jealous of Chora's life in another time. He'd only experienced eighteen years of life, and most of them he couldn't remember.

"How old are you?" He questioned with intrigue before realising it was wrong of him to ask a woman's age.

"One hundred and forty-four." Chora announced unashamedly.

David sprayed his mouthful of drink all over the floor and coughed on the remnants in his throat. It took him a good minute to catch his breath. Meanwhile, Chora had never laughed so hard in a long time, she was literally rolling on the floor holding her sides in a fit of laughter. When he finally could breathe again David had no choice but to join her in hysterics. They laughed for what seemed like hours. When the giggling finally did die off they both just lay on their backs looking up at the dusty ceiling above them.

"How did you end up a vamp?" David asked after a while.

Chora opened up the other bottle and took a swig.

"One night, John and I were sitting in bed when there was a knock at the front door. It was normally an emergency at that time of night. As we were getting up and re-dressed we suddenly heard screaming from downstairs, probably one of the servants. I was too scared to move but John left the bedroom to see what was happening. Next thing I know this man burst in, baring his teeth. He was so quick I couldn't stop him. He grabbed me and began feeding. John returned all bloody and beaten, but alive. He shot the vampire and I guess some of the vamp's blood maybe went into my mouth or got in my neck or something. The next day I died, but three days later. Voila." Chora took a huge swig of the bottle. It was half-way down already.

"Sorry to hear that. How did you end up with Libra?" David asked clearly enchanted by the series of events. He took another drink leaving a tiny bit left in the bottle. He was gutted it had run so low so quickly. Especially considering he had sprayed half the contents of the other bottle on the floor. As he lay back on his back he realised he was beginning to feel quite drunk.

"I managed to go without blood for a while, but the thirst eventually got the better of me." Chora admitted.

"You drank human blood?" David asked with a surprise that bordered disgust.

"Yeah, my first victim was a homeless drunk I found on a street corner, for a while he was the only one." Chora informed before polishing off the bottle. She rolled it away before looking up at the ceiling again.

"Nine people I killed, and I remember every single face, every scent, every scream." Chora said almost at the stage of tears. David didn't know what to say, so he didn't say anything at all. He just listened.

"I fed for a little under a year, that's when I met Winwood. He had traced the deaths to me and finally found me sleeping in an old barn. He woke me and told me I had two choices. Stop killing or be killed. It didn't seem like much of a choice at the time though..." Chora joked wiping a tear from her face with her right hand. David saw this and instinctively held her left hand, she held his hand back. From nowhere she leaned over and suddenly kissed him once on the lips. He looked deep into her deep blue teary eyes and kissed her back. Next thing he knew their lips were moving in an exhilarating snog, his first ever. He didn't know what to do as he felt her tongue slide into his mouth. He just lay there kissing her back like he thought he was supposed to, then as quick as it all started it ended.

"Sorry I can't." She said before getting up and running upstairs. Her long-flowing ginger hair following her up. David didn't know what to do or say, so he just lay there for a while recalling every beautiful moment of his first ever kiss. Eventually as he got tired he crawled up onto the dusty sofa and went to sleep.

CHAPTER 39

A WITCHES DUEL

Rachel was the weakest of the witches, but even she had trained hard enough to do basic magick with ease now. A bunch of attacking spells now formed part of her arsenal. Margaret was about the same level as Rachel. Nicole, however was much stronger than them both. As for Helena, she was almost at the same level as Holly even though Holly had had a couple of month head-start.

A lot of the spells the girls could do were now instantaneous, like a reflex. It actually annoyed Holly how easy Helena had picked everything up. She decided a friendly battle was in order just to put her back in her place a little bit. But before their witching duel, it was the turn of Rachel and Margaret. Nicole was instructed that she couldn't help and had to be a bystander in their shared body.

Helena's heart was in her mouth as she stood ready to watch. She was beginning to bond with Margaret, despite her shy and reserved nature. But she had also grown quite fond of Rachel over the time they had spent together, and as much as she hated to admit it to herself, there was a curious attraction there too.

"You ready?" Holly shouted as Rachel and Margaret stood facing each other.

"Yes." The pair replied in unison.

"Very well. Begin." Holly shouted at the pair.

Rachel started the duel by casting a smoke spell straight at Margaret. The aim was to blind her long enough to sneak round the back of her and pin her to the floor. As the smoke filled the air in front of her, Margaret countered with a light spell straight through the fogginess that fronted her. But she couldn't see Rachel ahead. Holly and Helena watched Rachel sneak round the side of the smoke towards the back of Margaret.

"She's coming..." Holly started to shout before Helena placed her hand over Holly's mouth.

"Just let them be." Helena interrupted with a smile.

It annoyed Holly rotten but she decided she would get her own back when they faced each other afterwards.

Margaret had heard Holly shout and was panning her light spell side to side in hope of a glimpse of Rachel, who by now was almost right around to Margaret's back. Unable to see, Margaret stood still listening for a moment, that's when she heard footsteps tiptoeing towards her from behind. She instinctively cast a fireball behind her without turning. Rachel only just managed to dodge it as it flew past her head and smouldered into ash on an adjacent wall. Rachel fired an ice spell at Margaret which she deflected onto one of the many metal columns supporting the roof. It froze and expanded on impact. Rachel fired another two in quick succession and used the distraction to and retreat back into the smoke. Margaret deflected both but had lost her opponent in the meantime.

"Not bad for newbies." Said a sudden yet familiar voice from beside Holly and Helena.

It was Elathan and he startled them both.

"Jesus. Can't you knock or ring a bell or something." Helena demanded trying to catch her breath.

"Or a mobile." Holly put in.

"Sorry." Elathan simply said. His gaze still transfixed on the fight in the background.

"Any news?" Holly asked while looking at him. His face was solemn and gaunt.

"A lot of changes going on below. Something big is happening. I want to do the spell in two weeks." Elathan put forth.

"That's not nearly enough time. We still have two sisters to get, and the ingredients. You know how hard they are gonna be." Holly commanded.

"Then you best get started right away."

"Why what's happened? Is mum okay?" Helena questioned.

But it was too late. Elathan had disappeared.

As Helena and Holly looked back towards the fight they couldn't make out much through the haze of smoke that remained. Only that one figure stood above another who was pinned to the floor.

"Alright you win, ger off." Rachel demanded.

It was clear Margaret had won the duel. While Margaret emerged from the smoke looking positively smug for once, Rachel sulkily held onto her wrist, it had been bent right back. Helena was about to ask if she was ok, but Rachel cut her off.

"Your turn." Rachel scowled as she passed the pair.

"Maybe next time." Holly replied with a smile.

"We have to go get Melissa now." Helena informed.

CHAPTER 40

WHAT'S YOUR POISON?

Chora and David pulled up outside of the Shorebank Wellness Centre for girls in the half-rusted Land-Rover Discovery. Chora was struggling through a massive head ache. David had one too, but he was dealing with his slightly better. The pair left the vehicle and headed over to the rusty old gates that barred their way. Chora pressed the bell and continued doing so until a hooded figure began making his way down the hilled pathway. One thing was sure as he made his way towards them, he certainly wasn't in any hurry. As the figure neared the gates David noticed big bushy eyebrows above an old looking face.

"Can I 'elp ya?" He asked after getting his breath back, the journey down had really took it out of him.

"We have a meeting with Mr Jewson." Chora said without looking at him. She was growing impatient, probably brought on by the hangover she was developing.

"Okay, calm down, I'm just doing my job." The old man exclaimed before fumbling with the gates locks. It took him a while but he got there. Chora felt guilty as he began locking the gate behind them.

"It's just up that hill, the building you're after is the one by itself just after the asylum. The two levelled one. I think he's expecting ya." The man said pointing in the general direction of where he meant.

David and Chora made their way up to it unaccompanied. As they reached their location David noticed a sign on the wall, it read:

"MR. JEWSON – HOSPITAL MANAGER"

"Look." He pointed it out to Chora. It was the first word they had shared since the kiss the night before. Things were now awkward between them, but David had no idea why. He enjoyed the drink and the kiss from what he could remember, he hoped he hadn't done it wrong. Chora didn't reply, instead she gave a big knock on the door. It wasn't long until a balding middle-aged overweight man answered the door. He adjusted his glasses while looking at them.

"Can I help you?" He asked curiously.

"We are here about the incident." Chora informed squeezing her eyes shut as the sun shone over the hill and into her eyes.

"You don't look like police." Mr Jewson said while inspecting David.

"Branch of." Chora simply put.

"What sorry?" Mr Jewson asked as he finished looking at David.

"We are a separate branch of..."

"...If you say so. I will just get my coat." He interrupted before disappearing out of sight.

He returned several minutes later, he clearly wasn't ashamed to keep his guests waiting.

With that they left the doorway of the smaller building for the hospital wing. It was a grand building and was probably a manor in its previous life. All eighty-four of its front windows contained white sheets and were boarded up with metal bars. The bricked front had numerous colours which looked like it had been extended numerous times. Ugly looking gargoyles sat idly across the entire rooftop sill. It was just as foreboding inside as it was out. The trio ventured through several locked chambers before they arrived at a normal looking room. Mr Jewson opened it to reveal a cell with padded walls. Chora and David followed him in.

"They escaped from in here." Mr Jewson said through gritted teeth. He was obviously still very annoyed about it.

"The door is the only way in and out?" Chora asked while looking around the room.

"Obviously." Mr Jewson said before looking at his watch. "Be right back." He said before disappearing. He didn't wait for a response.

"Keep an eye out." Chora said to David before pulling out her EMF. David watched Jewson disappear into one of the many side rooms then watched the empty hallway as Chora scanned the room. Towards the back of the room the EMF was spiking a full red. It caught David's attention and he temporarily looked away from the hallway. When he looked back down it Mr Jewson was already halfway back.

"He's back Chora." David said as quickly and quietly as possible. It was just enough notice for her to hide the EMF back in her right-side jeans pocket. When Mr Jewson returned he knew something was amiss, he was always being shifty so he could easily spot it in somebody else. He didn't like being in the dark in his own kingdom and something seemed to suddenly shift in his whole persona.

"Follow me." He demanded through gritted teeth. Beads of sweat began to form on his brow.

He escorted the pair to a room on the outside of the building that was part kitchen, part office, an aroma of cheap microwave meals filled the air and told them it was probably used as a staff room. He looked around the room frantically for something. It obviously wasn't a room he often visited. He spotted what he was after.

"Water? Of course, you want water, how rude of me not to ask. You will conduct staff interviews here. I will send them in for you. Now water."

Mr Jewson headed over to the water dispenser and made sure his back blocked their view of what he was doing. Chora and David were too busy clearing the lime coloured table of food wrappers and old cups of tea to notice Mr Jewson fill a cup from the dispenser, insert a tablet and stir the cup with his finger until it dissolved. He did the same with the second cup and returned to the table placing them central to the pair. Chora took one look then downed it like it was the last resource in the world. David took a sip then sat down beside her. Mr Jewson could barely hide his smirk as he left the room in search of his largest staff members.

David just sat there in silence for a time while Chora seemed to be distracted by something. He was confused by her strange actions; he went to get her another drink of water when she grabbed his hand.

"Don't. I think it's been poisoned." Chora announced while trying to figure out what the strange taste in her mouth was.

"Why would he try and poison us? We came to help him." David asked confused.

"I don't know, but you have to get me out of here now." Chora demanded while trying to get up from her chair, it was a struggle. David helped her to the door; he turned the handle of the door with his free left hand and was surprised to find it open. They left the room as David looked up and down the corridor. To the left three guards and Mr Jewson were on their way. They sped up as they noticed the pair leaving. To the right was the exit, barred by a single locked door.

"Kick it open, quick." Chora ushered as she leaned against a nearby wall for support. Three kicks and the door rocked open on its one remaining hinge. The guards were in quick pursuit as David and Chora made their way outside and down the bank. Halfway down it was apparent they weren't going to make it. The anger on Mr Jewson's face began to grow into a smile.

"You'll have to fight them, I will manage." Chora said pushing David free of her. "Just don't kill them." She shouted back as she began crawling along the pathway towards the locked gate. David wanted to flee with her, he was too scared to fight, even if it was against humans.

The guards pulled out baton sticks from their belts while Mr Jewson readied a syringe and they approached David. David was about to run away but the first swing was already on its way. He blocked it with ease, and the second and the third. His confidence grew as h blocked and dodged each and every shot. But the men grew frustrated and he grew tired. Then a smack across his face stunned him and knocked him to the floor. He got back up blocking another strike, but then another blow cracked against his back, and then another across his arm.

As he began to get overpowered by the guards Mr Jewson carefully approached him armed with a needle and an evil grin. David took a knee as he felt another smack across the face and then his shoulder. The guards surrounded him ready to pin him down so Jewson could stick the needle in.

"David. Run." Chora shouted back from the other side of the fence.

David took another a strike to his back and arm as he squeezed through an opening and bolted away. He ran as hard as his legs could carry him as the guards chased him in pursuit. One swift jump and he was over the fence. The guards pulled to a stop astounded that David had jumped an impossible jump. David was relieved as Chora pulled away. Mr Jewson was so angry, he just stood there with his fists clenched for ten whole minutes. As he began to feel a pain in his right hand he looked down to see he had crushed the syringe and was covered in blood, glass and a dark yellow liquid.

CHAPTER 41

MELISSA

The journey across Newcastle was a silent one. None of the sisters would admit it but they were all feeling a little nervous. Yet each metro station that was ticked off by the announcer was a welcome declaration. They alighted the cab together and surged with the hustle and bustle onto the street. It was around 9PM and the day crowd was clearing for the night brigade of drinkers and bouncers. The calm before the storm, the clean before the mess. The four girls stayed close to avoid the attention of the early starters, the bottom feeders of social drinking. A few winding streets and Greggs bakeries later and they stood ahead of their location. The pub "The Grey Goose."

It was single story pub, very old and very selective with its guests. If they weren't girls, they probably wouldn't have gotten in. The sisters huddled into the corner out of sight, while Rachel got the drinks in and looked around for Melissa. On her return journey, she spotted her dressed in a black biker jacket on the other side of the pub. As Rachel put the four pints of lager down she informed the girls what she had found.

"She is playing pool with a bunch of bikers."

"Really lager?" Helena joked.

But after a sip she found it quite refreshing.

"I didn't know what anyone liked." Rachel defended.

"It's fine, thanks." Holly said taking a big gulp.

Margaret took a drink because she didn't want to feel left out, but she clearly didn't enjoy it. One drink down and its subsequent toilet trip later and the girls were ready to make their move. The plan was to lure her outside, tell her the truth and with any luck she would just agree to join them. Holly approached solo while the other girls stood nearby ready to back her up.

"Hi I think you're my sister." Holly said lamely, removing the dyed-purple hair that was restricting her face. She wished she had come up with something better to say. But the truth was, she hadn't really thought this part through. By this point, she wished she had given this job to somebody else.

"Who me?" Melissa (who's jet black hair matched her black biker apparel) replied without looking up from her next shot on the pool table.

"Yes, I'm Holly. You are Melissa right?"

"Only child. Scram." Melissa said before taking the shot.

As if her words were orders, one of her burly bald biker-friends stood in front of Holly blocking her from Melissa's eye sight.

"Just look at me and you will see the similarities Melissa." Holly tried to counter around the width of the biker man, but he moved as she did. Intrigued Melissa looked up, her view was blocked.

"Show me." She announced all blasé, as if this scene was a regular occurrence for her.

As the biker stood to one side to reveal Holly, Melissa's face turned to shock, then intrigue, then panic.

Quicker than any of the girls had time to react she was out of the back door of the pub. All of the girls followed her in hot pursuit. Piercing eyes following them all out the door. The sisters and Rachel broke into a sprint as they followed Melissa down the back lane and around the corner. After a good amount of running, enough to wear Margaret down so much she had to switch with Nicole, they all come to a stop at a massive football field. Melissa glided over the small wooden fence and towards the centre of the pitch. Here in the middle of nowhere they were out of relative eyeshot and earshot and Melissa could defend herself with magick. The girls cautiously made their way towards her.

"What do you want?" Melissa shouted when they were near enough.

"For you to come with us." Holly replied painting for breath.

"What are you? Doppelgangers? Here to replace me?"

"No. We need your help." Helena reasoned. She had a feeling this was going to turn into a duel.

The scene was now set like a modern-day cowboy film. Four people surrounding one. For a minute, they all just stood looking at each other ready to attack. It was Melissa that made the first move. Lighting cracked from the sky hitting Nicole straight in the chest knocking her flying through the air. Not to be outdone, Holly fired one back which Melissa deflected away with ease. Helena cast a vine spell, a load of roots shot out of the ground around her and began wrapping themselves around Melissa. She broke free and floated up into the air above them, but they grew with her, one reaching up and wrapping itself around her foot.

Rachel, who had sneaked up on Melissa from behind, was now just a few yards away when Melissa burnt the vines around her to a crisp. Another lightning bolt by Holly was dispatched as easy as the first, and another. Helena ran over to help Nicole up as Holly tried to keep Melissa busy. By this time, Rachel was right behind her. Rachel waited patiently as Melissa floated back down to the floor, oblivious of her surroundings.

As Melissa's feet touched the grass of the football field Rachel grabbed her pulling her to the floor. She wrapped her arms around her waist as tightly as she could and held on for dear life. Rachel felt Melissa's skin burn red hot, yet still she held on. As an electric shock by Holly ripped through both their bodies, still she held on. As tiny little spikes protruded from Melissa skin piercing Rachel's arms, still she held on. The freezing cold that came next was a welcome relief on the second-degree burns, and the piercing pains she had already suffered.

But as Melissa's skin burnt hot again Rachel's grip began to loosen. Just as she let go Helena, Holly and Nicole all combined an electricity spell that knocked Melissa out cold.

"You okay?" Holly asked Rachel as she picked her up from the floor. Rachel didn't speak because she couldn't find the words. Her whole body pulsed with pain. When Helena arrived and cuddled her, Rachel just stood there, tears streaming down her face forming a puddle on her top.

"Thankyou." Helena said kissing Rachel softly on the lips.

Rachel was in too much pain to kiss her back. She just stood there silently shivering. Thankfully Holly was able to provide some temporary relief with a soothing spell. Nothing permanent could be done until she was back with her spell books. The girls ordered a taxi and waited without a word.

As Nicole and Holly carried Melissa's unconscious body into a taxi they were surprised to find its driver wasn't the least bit suspicious. He only looked at her twice for the full 30-minute journey home, and that was just to make sure she hadn't been sick in his cab. Helena sat with Rachel for the whole journey, slowly rubbing her back to try and take her mind off the pain in her front. Once the taxi driver was paid, the girls began carrying Melissa towards the factory.

CHAPTER 42

DOOR TO DOOR

Doc and Celeste were already quite drunk, but so far, it was for nothing. Not a snippet of information, nobody had seen or heard a single thing. With all but one of Sunderland's supernatural hotspots already visited, they found themselves heading to their final destination. It was Doc's least favourite drinking haunt Ah-Pla. The loud music, flashing lights, haze of cigarette smoke and stink of teenagers were just a few of the reasons he hated the place.

Celeste was a familiar face to the bouncers and they got straight in. The pair bumped their way through the busy entrance and down several flights of stairs to its underground basement. Once inside they immediately made their way to the bar. Most of its stools sat idle. Only two types of people sat there, alcoholics and the law. Doc was about to sit until Celeste pulled him away to one of the free aisles around the outside of the room. It didn't take long for a long legged blonde woman with barely any clothes on to approach them. It didn't take her long to grow impatient.

"What would ya like?" She said in the fakest American accent Doc had ever heard.

"What is there?" He asked shrugging his shoulders.

"You can order food, drinks, a lap dance, drugs, anything within reason." The woman quickly informed, she didn't want to be seen talking to the same group for too long.

Celeste ordered two pints of house ale and a chat with the manager if he was free. She cited "mutually beneficial business" to peak his interest.

Their drinks were drunk by the time the manager arrived. He was a tall fellow, a little on the rotund side wearing a snazzy suit with sunglasses. He approached armed with a false grin as if he was pleased for their custom. Truth was, he hated new faces. Regulars were predictable.

"Mr Falstaff." Celeste said offering her hand as a greeting, one he ignored. You didn't have to be a bar owner to recognise his permanently smug face, he had fingers in many pies.

"I'm afraid you have me at a disadvantage, Celeste is it?" Mr Falstaff said taking a seat beside them in the aisle.

"It doesn't matter what my name is, we are here on official Libra business." Celeste said before motioning to Doc. It took him a few seconds to get it, but when he did he pulled out his I.D to show the man. Mr Falstaff recoiled as if allergic to what he was being shown. An angry set of vampire teeth glistened in the neon lights. He then got up laughing.

"It'll take more than a stupid badge to scare me."

He turned his back to walk away. Thankfully Celeste was quick.

"True, but can you say the same for all your customers. Will they still feel comfortable drinking in the same establishment as a few cops, maybe several?"

He turned ready to strike, he managed to cool himself before he made a silly move. There were too many witnesses to get away with killing a cop. He instead put a single hand in the air. Within seconds a few of his barely dressed barmaids were around him. He took his seat again. Girl after girl brought drink after drink until the table was full with a varied range. Mr Falstaff picked a drink at random and downed it to show this wasn't a poisonous trick.

"On the house." He gestured. "Now, what do you want?" He words were put across kindly, but you could taste the hate in them.

"Thank you, and don't worry, we just want you to answer a few harmless questions." Celeste confirmed before picking up one of the drinks and taking a long sip.

"Shoot." Mr Falstaff offered.

"We wanna know if you recognise any of these." Doc asked pulling out an envelope of photos from his inner jacket. Mr Falstaff poured them into his left hand and started going through them. They were all CCTV shots from Priveam of the people that took over the bar.

Mr Falstaff went through them slowly.

"Nah sorry." He said putting them back in the envelope and handing them back to Doc. Doc gave him a disapproving look.

"Honestly, I ain't seen any of them in my life..." Falstaff pleaded. "...Believe me, my business comes before any one vamp." He added.

Doc and Celeste looked disappointed, but they believed him. Celeste finished her drink before grabbing a pen and paper and writing down her number before giving it to Falstaff.

"If you see or hear anything in the meantime let us know yeah."

"Will do." The man said before snatching the paper and disappearing into the crowd of rowdy partygoers. Doc and Celeste left quickly after.

Meanwhile, the barman who had been observing them with suspicion all night watched them leave. As soon as they were out of sight he moved upstairs through the staff entrance until the trance music was barely audible. He pulled his phone out and dialled 'Cerevad'. It took a while, but there was an answer.

"Yes." Cerevad answered.

"I've just seen Celeste, what happened?"

"There was an unforeseen complication."

"What now?" The barman demanded. His voice broke with worry.

"We move to Plan B. Kill her if you see her." Said the voice on the other end of the phone.

The barman didn't have a chance to answer, his head had been cleanly sliced away from the rest of body. It rolled along the hallway like a broken bowling ball. His remaining frame fell to the floor in a spray of blood revealing his assailant, a woman dressed entirely in yellow with a sword for a forearm. She produced a fake arm from her black duffel bag and clicked it in place over the top of the sword. With her working hand, she bent down and picked up the phone that had fallen to the floor.

"Hello." She said through a smile.

"Is that you?" The voice hesitated.

"Yes. You're next."

Cerevad pleaded excuses on the other end of the phone, but it was no good, the phone was on the floor and the woman was gone.

*****

Meanwhile, Torus and Trigger had been following Tom around for the entire day. It was proving more and more likely that he didn't have anything to do with Helena's disappearance. He couldn't even cover up his affair properly, never mind a missing person.

CHAPTER 43

HOME FOR NOW

By the time Rose returned from Scotland the following day, Anthony was feeling loads better. He couldn't move very fast or in awkward angles, but other than that he was absolutely fine. Rose come back to explain to an excited Anthony that they had a new lead to follow, one she was promised would lead to answers about vampires. Deep down they both knew their search, for Anthony's best friend David and Rose's sister Daisy, was probably going to lead down yet more dangerous roads. But that wasn't going to stop either of them from continuing.

As Rose dropped Anthony off at home, they both agreed to have the weekend off to heal and then continue their work on Monday. As you would expect Anthony's mother Wendy and his crazy aunt were absolutely ecstatic to see him, then cross at his disappearance, then grateful he was alive, then cross again and so on. Her emotions were giving him whiplash. But it was nice to normalise again, if only for a few days.

By the Sunday he needed to be free of the house. He went alone for some lunch and grabbed some gaming magazines on the way back. Upon his return home, he was so enthralled in the magazines that he neglected to notice the car that was sat opposite his house, its occupants waiting for him. The two people in the car eagerly watched his mother and aunt (dressed to the nines) leave for the night via a taxi, leaving Anthony home alone. They patiently waited another five hours for his bedroom light to switch off and then another thirty minutes before they got out the car and checked up and down the street. One of them pulled out a series of tools and within two minutes he had lock-picked his way inside.

Once the door was closed behind them they listened intently for noise, the only break of silence was the snoring coming from upstairs. They tip-toed their way up the stairs and towards the source of the snoring, the door was ajar but not enough to fit straight inside. It creaked as they forced their way through, but it wasn't enough to stir Anthony, who's snoring was now full-throttle on the bed. One of the two men approached the headboard quickly and quietly, and was just centimetres away when the other man removed a gun and pointed it at Anthony's half-dressed body. Legitus gave Ryan a nod to say he was ready and he lunged with his hands. He placed the base of his palms on either side of Anthony's head. He inhaled deeply again before invading Anthony's thoughts.

Images and sounds flashed through Legitus' head. There was a giant pink frog with fangs eating from a red jam river. The river flowed into a giant waterfall that was falling over the top a giant tombstone. The tombstone belonged to David Sixsmith. Legitus breathed out, then pressed again. This time he flowed from Anthony's dreams into his memories. He saw Anthony in a newsagent, then eating dinner. He sped through the days he had spent at home. Suddenly he was in a car with a woman driving backwards, then he was in a bed covered in bandages. Legitus breathed out and rewound some more, he continued on and on until he got to when he needed to be, Priveam. Legitus watched the memory, then rewinded and watched it again. Before speeding backwards once more, minutes becoming hours, hours becoming days. Legitus skipped the funeral, skipped the grief that came before it and landed bang in Anthony's room. He was playing video games, with David by his side. Legitus slowly pulled away, he had everything he needed.

"Well?" Ryan whispered.

"I will tell you in the car, quick let's go." Legitus said before they both tip-toed downstairs.

Just as they got out of the house and across the street a taxi pulled up outside of Anthony's house, it was his mother and aunty giggling loudly in the silent street. Legitus and Ryan jumped into the car and drove off.

"What is it? What did you see?" Ryan asked impatiently as they turned another corner.

"He's David's best friend. Probably the one he's been asking about."

"Our David? What does he know so far?" Ryan queried.

"That vamps exist and that David is either one of them, or was killed by one..." Legitus said with a smile, he was impressed. "...Him and some copper woman aren't too far away from finding out the truth, not too shabby for humans." Legitus joked.

"Oy none of that." Ryan scoffed back.

CHAPTER 44

SISTER TO SISTER

Melissa woke up tied to a chair. She looked around the room to get her bearings. It appeared to be some sort of abandoned factory. The smell of damp lined the air, no ascertainable fixtures or machinery. She could hear quiet talking but there was nobody in sight. Melissa tried to burn the bonds that tied her down, when nothing happened she looked down and noticed the sigil on the floor that was preventing her from doing any spell. It was old magick, no way around it. She was stuck, for now at least. Melissa traced her memories. She remembered the duel with the mirrored faces, the witches posing as sisters she didn't have.

She was busy trying to wriggle free from her bonds when four girls walked into the room. Three of them had an eerily similar face to her own, all of them with different hair colours. The one with bleach blonde hair looked angry, like she wanted Melissa dead. The one with ginger hair looked tense, like she was ready for a fight. The one with purple hair looked rather pleased with herself. A fourth (unsimilar-looking) girl stood back as if she was scared of Melissa.

"You'd better let me go or I will call a daemon to strange you all." Melissa threatened.

Holly and Helena laughed aloud, they either knew it was an empty threat or they didn't care. The other two girls tried their best to hide their growing fear.

"What do you want?" Melissa tried instead. She had never been in this position. She had never felt so weak or exposed. It was frustrating to say the least.

"We already told you who we are, we need your help." Helena reiterated.

"I'm Holly, this is Margaret slash Nicole and that's Helena." Holly said introducing the sisters. She waited patiently for a reply, there wasn't one. Rachel waited patiently for her introduction which also never arrived. Melissa's eyes were too busy darting around the room to take anything in.

"So, you're supposed to be my sisters?" Melissa questioned as a distraction to gain more time to find an escape route.

"Yes." Holly said kindly. She hoped Melissa was finally coming around.

"You see, I know for a fact my mam and dad died in a car crash when I was five, cos I was there. And because I remember being stuck in numerous care homes 'til I was FUCKING FOURTEEN!" Melissa frustratingly squealed. There was no weakness in the bonds tying her to the chair.

"I'm sorry to hear that, I truly am. But they must have been your adoptive parents." Helena sympathised moving towards her.

"You are not my sister." Melissa barked trying to move her chair away from Helena.

"Yes, she is." Came a man's voice from behind the girls. It was Elathan.

"Elathan?" Melissa said in shock as she noticed who it was.

The girls were stunned into silence. The fact a daemon just appeared in the factory was nothing. The fact he knew Melissa, and Melissa knew him was the kicker. He calmly walked over to her and began untying the bonds that bound her wrists to the chair arms. Everyone was on edge, not sure what to do next.

"Are they really?" Melissa whispered to make sure it wasn't just a ploy to get free.

"Yeah, they…" Elathan began.

"Wait. Wait. Wait." Helena interrupted. "…How do you two…?" Helena asked as Elathan unbound the final piece of rope that wrapped her left ankle to the chair leg.

"I haven't got very long, quick make a circle." Elathan said wiping down any sweat from his palms onto his jeans. The sisters moved closer to each other, Rachel just stood there confused as to whether she was included in his command.

"You too Rachel, your part of this coven now whether you like it or not." Elathan said as he opened his palms for the girls either side of him to hold his hands.

"Everybody hold hands and close your eyes." He instructed as they formed a perfect circle while holding onto each other. As Helena and Rachel held hands they closed their eyes so none of them noticed the other was smiling. Their cozied grip a little more meaningful than everybody else's.

As the circle completed, the same images began to flash through all of their minds as they shared consciousness through Elathan. To begin with it was each other's memories. Recent at first. Then random memories, then very specific ones. A young Melissa being beaten by a much older and bigger girl at a care home. Margaret and Nicole fighting over who had control of the body. Helena getting married in a beautiful church on a lovely sunny day. Rachel slitting her wrists because she was so ashamed of being a lesbian. Holly on Christmas day opening the first of her 137 presents. Elathan carefully removing a man's skin from his body, the person was bound to the table and screaming in agony.

Suddenly the face of a woman appeared. Nobody had to say anything, the sisters knew it was their mother Emily. They all watched with grimace and astonishment as she gave birth to six adorable little girls, sextuplets. The last of them was Margaret and she was still-born. A woman the girls didn't recognise took away the still born, another woman followed her out carrying Nicole. They returned with one baby. Margaret's soul had obviously been put inside Nicole's body. They all cried as they watched their own history enfold before them.

The images suddenly fast forwarded to Emily going through countless spell books in search of an answer, she didn't want her babies to have to share a body. She was up all day and all night looking for items, clues, spells, anything that might help. Then one day she used the last resort she had, a crossroads daemon. But the daemon she called was greedy, he wanted more than her soul, so much more.

The daemon betrayed her into killing herself and leaving her babies behind. The daemon would have had their souls too, but their father gave his babies away before the daemon had a chance to return. When the daemon tortured the Dad, he could say with honesty he didn't know where they were. He had lost his babies, but he had saved them at the same time. As the memories ended, a flood of tears streamed down all the girls faces as they opened their eyes.

"What was her name?" Melissa asked quickly wiping her face dry.

"Her name is Emily and we are breaking her out of Hell. You in?" Holly asked with hope.

"Damn right, who's missing?" Melissa asked as they all smiled, clearly pleased to have her on board.

"Alyson." Holly noted.

"We're ready to go when Rachel is." Helena informed releasing Rachel's hand as she realised she still had hold.

"You're the one that kept hold of me yeah?" Melissa asked looking towards Rachel.

"Yeah sorry about that." Rachel shyly put in.

"No need. Pleasure to have you on board." Melissa said hugging Rachel. "And sorry about your skin, are you okay?"

"Yes, much better thanks to Holly." Rachel said with a smile. She was a bit embarrassed by all the attention, but it was the first time she felt part of the group, the first time she felt accepted. It was also the first time she had felt at home in a long time.

"You coming with..." Melissa turned to ask Elathan, but he was gone.

"Don't worry he always does that." Holly said as they all began laughing aloud.

CHAPTER 45

MOVING ON

David awoke to a blue light flashing within his room alarm system. It meant a meeting had been called. His body still ached from the beating he got the day before so he could get not ready as fast as he would have liked. He painfully made his way to the meeting room and was pleased to find that Winwood had brought in Cannibal Café Coffee's for everyone. David picked up and tasted one of the many Mosquito Mocha's that sat around the table, it was the perfect pick-me-up, even without the squirrel blood and hazelnut syrup David had chosen to drink last time.

"We are about to get very busy, I need to know what you've all been doing and everything you've found out. Anyone wanna start?" Winwood asked grabbing a pen and paper to take notes.

Torus stuck his hand up first before speaking.

"As you know, me and Trigger were sent to follow Tom, Helena's husband, to see if he had anything to do with her disappearance." Torus put forward.

"And…" Winwood gestured.

"And I very much doubt he, or his mistress, had anything to do with it. He can't even hide his affair very well never mind a murder, or kidnapping." Torus said.

"There is no way, the blokes just useless." Trigger added sending the whole group into hysterics.

"And the girlfriend?" Winwood questioned.

"She is anarl." Trigger answered to a bigger rupture of laughter.

When the giggling finally settled down Winwood spoke.

"Right next aim then, do a full evaluation and history on Helena. Birth to present day. Get everything you can on her. Right who's next?"

"Speaking of useless people, that Mr Jewson wasn't much help either..." Chora started. "...Me and David were sent to check out the psychiatric hospital at Shorebank, where if you remember, three girls disappeared. We got there to do an investigation and he tried to frigging poison us."

Everybody looked shocked and waited for the rest of the story with bated breath.

"Thankfully, the little fight training that David did have, was enough to get us out of there." Chora complimented.

A round of congratulations was aimed at David making him feel a little silly, but the pain he was in now felt worthwhile.

"Did you manage to get anything from the disappearance, or did he poison you on arrival?" Winwood joked.

"The EMF spiked a full-red in the room that they disappeared from, but if he is throwing poison around willy-nilly, the place could just be haunted." Chora reasoned.

"Right, make an anonymous tip to the police about him and just forget about that case. You two can train together in the meantime." Winwood finalised before crossing something out on his paper.

David was pleased he would be spending more time with Chora, even if it did feel a bit awkward since their kiss.

"Okay next." Winwood motioned.

"Me and Celeste didn't get anything from the bars I'm afraid." Doc added.

"I heard someone was murdered there last night." Winwood informed.

"Yeah, but it was after we were there, and murder is a regular occurrence in the club unfortunately. Probably coincidental." Doc hoped.

"It's a rough club full of rough people to be fair." Winwood sympathised.

Winwood took some more notes. He looked a little lost. All of his leads so far lead exactly nowhere.

"Are Apex on the murder case then, or do you want us to look at it?" Doc asked feeling partly responsible.

"Apex are already on it. But it might be worth having a chat with one of them, see if there are any links with any of our cases." Winwood put back.

David put his hand up to stop the meeting for a second. "Sorry. Who are Apex?"

"The vamp government." Winwood answered before proceeding to explain. "It has five arms. The Vampire Royal Guard, which is basically the army. Then there's the police and law which governs how we will and punishes those that disobey the laws. The other three are blood management, disaster control and the press.

All of them are ran by the Royals. The only real power in the vamp world." Winwood informed.

"Wait. I thought we were the police."

"We basically are, but they get all the high profile and easy cases, anything they can use as a power play or publicity stunt. We get the..."

"...Shit" Doc put in.

"For want of a better word, yes." Winwood added.

The group giggled at the stupidity of it all before getting back to the meeting at hand.

"Right, Legitus. Ryan. What about you guys? Did you read that humans memories?" Winwood asked looking rather deflated by his lack of results.

Legitus and Ryan looked at each other, not sure what to say or do. Legitus considered bringing an end to the meeting, to bring this matter up privately with Winwood. He thought carefully before he answered.

"We were sent to find out who the humans were, the ones involved in a bar fight at Priveam when we arrived. It turns out it was some police woman called Rose, and David's friend Anthony."

The room was stunned silent, no-one more so than David. He was completely lost for words, the rest of the room sat quietly observing his reaction. Only Winwood dared to speak.

"You remember what I said to you David?" He asked.

David either didn't hear him speak, or was too busy trying to process what he had just been told.

"You remember what I told you David?" Winwood said louder.

"Erm…yeah… He can't know about us, but if he finds out on his own accord." David answered nonchalantly, but he couldn't hide the worry, or the excitement from his words.

His brain quickly flashed through dozens of future possibilities, both good and bad.

"Is he in danger?" David asked in concern.

"Yes…" Winwood replied honestly. "…but Ryan is going to follow them to try and figure out what they know so far."

"But…" David tried.

"If they put themselves in harm's way, Ryan will bring them here." Winwood sympathised. "But if they give up on their search on their own accord, you must give up hope, because then there is nothing more I can do."

"Thanks." David said. It was probably the best he could hope for. He just hoped it all ended well.

The whole revelation about Anthony pleased David, but it generated more questions and worry than anything else. The room was quiet for a while. Nobody was sure what to say or do next. Winwood broke the silence with another announcement.

"In final news, we have a royal guest visiting next week." Winwood informed happily.

"Which one is it?" Trigger asked with intrigue as the room finally settled down.

"We honestly don't know who yet. All we were informed is that they will be staying with us for a week and we have to make sure our security is tight and up to date. Two of the VRG will be coming to check it the day before. I guess we might find out then."

By the afternoon, the attitude in the base was upbeat again. Ryan had gone to keep an eye David's friend Anthony (David had asked to go but wasn't allowed in case he was seen). Trigger and Winwood were busy assessing all the security in the base, testing annoyingly loud alarms and stuff. Paige and Legitus were spring-cleaning, Doc and Torus were busy planning a banquet for the Royal arrival. David and Celeste were busy sparring. Everything hurt but he was determined not take such a beating in future.

CHAPTER 46

A PACK OF LIES

Anthony woke up with a stotting headache and blurred vision, it was as if his head had been crushed by something while he slept, his dreams were so vivid and for a while he wasn't sure if he was actually awake, or just dreaming that he had awoken. Eventually he begrudgingly got up and showered. He was fully dressed by the time he realised he had a text from Rose saying she was on her way.

Anthony nearly screamed as he looked outside the window and saw her car waiting. He hurried downstairs, put his trainers on, and shouted "Love you, bye." to his mother in the sitting room. His mother was too busy nursing a hangover to go after him. She simply shouted it back at him, but it was to lame and late for him to hear it. His mother barely found the energy to turn around and look out the window as the car, with him in it, pulled away.

"You haven't waited long, have you?" Anthony worried as he adjusted his seat and put his seat belt on.

"No. No. Just got here a couple of minutes ago." Rose lied.

There was an awkward silence for a while. None of them knew what to say, but when they both thought of something they spoke at the same time.

"How have you…?" Anthony began.

"What you been…?" Rose started.

They both giggled.

"You first?" Anthony insisted.

"What have you been up to? And how's your ribs?" Rose asked.

"Fine actually. I think the bruising has gone." Anthony replied. It was then he noticed the bandage still wrapped around Rose's right hand. "How's your hand?"

"Painful, but I have full use of it."

After a quick stop for hot drinks, the pair found themselves engrossed in conversation. It was like they had known each other for years and hadn't seen each other in months. They were so pre-occupied with each other, neither of them so much as suspected they had been followed to their destination. They had drove for just under an hour to get to the block of run down flats they had come for. Ryan pulled over a few cars behind them and pretended to send a text as Anthony and Rose got out of the car. Anthony was shocked as Rose pulled out a gun in broad daylight, he was even more shocked as she handed it over to him. It was a Walther P99 handgun, half black, half brown.

"It's just a precaution, we nearly died last time." Rose insisted.

He paused for a moment, things had just got very serious. Then he remembered the reason he was here, David.

"Ok. How do you use it?" Anthony asked.

Rose took it back off him.

"Safety is on the top…" She explained as she showed him. "It won't fire when the safety is on." She attempted to press the trigger a couple of times, Anthony was grateful it didn't budge. She handed it back over, he took it carefully, as it were a grenade that could blow up at any moment.

"Once the safety is off pull the barrel back at the top, aim and fire. It's got twelve rounds in the clip. I've got more ammo if you need it, but that should do for now."

"Okay. Safety. Barrel. Aim and fire. Simple." Anthony croaked.

"Don't use it unless its life and death. You ready?" Rose asked as she locked the car.

"Yeah." Anthony said before breathing a deep breath, putting the gun in the back of his jeans and following her across the road.

Rose pulled a crumpled piece of paper out from her pocket and matched it with the weather-worn street sign attached to the corner of the first block of flats, it was a match. Rose yanked the heavy front-door open and walked in with Anthony by her side. Ryan followed them over but stood outside watching them through the glass of the front entrance. Rose walked over and pressed the buzzer by the empty main reception. It wasn't long until a hulk of a man came scuffling to their assistance panting like an out of breath dog, he smelled like one too.

"Hi, James Blackstock sent me…" Rose said before going to show him the paper. He snatched it from her before she had a chance. He took a mere glance at it then dropped it on the floor.

"Follow me." He said leaving the messy reception area and walking towards the lift. They shrugged their shoulders and followed him inside. He pressed 'B' and down they went. The lift eventually pinged open to reveal a long dark corridor. It was so dark you couldn't see the other side. The man pointed into the darkness, grunted and pushed them out of the lift.

"Alright." Rose fumed.

The lift doors closed behind them plunging the already poorly-lit corridor into complete darkness. Thankfully they both had mobile phones to light the way forward.

As the lift doors pinged open, the receptionist was annoyed to see somebody else was now at the reception area, it was Ryan.

"James Blackstock sent me." Ryan tried with the same piece of paper he had picked up from the floor.

He was surprised to find it worked and soon found himself in the same darkened corridor as Anthony and Rose, only he stupidly didn't bring a gun.

CHAPTER 47

ALYSON

It was a whole week before the sisters managed to track Alyson down. It was a drab and damp Sunday evening when Holly, Nicole, Melissa, Helena and Rachel found themselves impatiently sat behind her in a stolen Jeep. She was in a police car ahead of them. She had been arrested for assault and was currently on her way to a police station. The girls were busy arguing over the best way to spring her free when the police car forced them to stop at a traffic light. It stayed red for an awfully long time, much longer than it was meant to. It then got to the point where everyone knew it should have changed by now. Something had paused it on the stop sign.

The girls watched with intrigue as one of the two arresting officers left the car to check it out. The girls couldn't see inside the car very well but a sudden flash of light gave away that something had just happened inside the car. The other officer turned to see what was happening when he was sent flying through the air before eventually landing on an elegantly displayed flowerbed. The ridiculously overpriced council installation was immediately ruined as it took his brute force. The girls got out of the Jeep as Alyson got out of the car. She burned the steel handcuffs so hot they burned white before they fell to the floor with a lame thud.

"Alyson." Holly shouted at the green-haired lookalike as she turned to walk away.

She quickly spun on heel and fired an ice spell. Luckily for Holly, Helena was ready and managed to deflect it against a nearby lamp-post. The steel frame immediately froze over from top to bottom.

"Holly?" Alyson asked curious. It was then that she noticed the rest of the girls. She recognised them all, except one. The girls didn't understand how she knew who they were. They hadn't even explained themselves yet.

Suddenly from nowhere an arrow came flying through the air plunging straight into Alyson's chest from behind the girls. They turned in shock to see who had fired the shot. Rapidly approaching the girls was a group of seven people dressed entirely in black, they looked like ninjas. They leaped and barrelled over the street furniture with athletic easy as they headed towards Alyson. Helena was first to react. She fired a lightning bolt straight at the nearest assailant, the air cracked with its power lighting up most of the street. She quickly barked orders at the rest of the girls.

"Nicole, Rachel, get Alyson to the Jeep. Holly, Melissa, you're with me." Helena commanded.

As the man Helena had struck with a lightning bolt hit a nearby wall, he struggled to get back up. His fellow attackers gave the girls a look of disdain and changed their focus to them instead. A hail of arrows and anger quickly filled the air as Nicole and Rachel grabbed Alyson. She was still alive, but she was impaled and losing blood fast. Her complexion looked pale against the backdrop of her neon green bob-cut.

Melissa turned the arrows to ash before firing a couple of fireballs directly at their attackers, none of them hit the target. Holly only just managed to dodge the swing of a Sabre sword from one of the men before she levitated a nearby rock through his skull. The attackers were fast as they drew in from all sides. Rachel helped Nicole put Alyson into the back of the Jeep before running around to the driver's seat to start it up. She hadn't even noticed one of the assassins sneak right up to the window. He drove his sword straight at Rachel's neck. Lucky for her, Elathan had skipped between the pair, taking the full length of the blade through his abdomen. As Elathan smoked out Helena sent the ninja flying through the air with such a speed that when he hit the brick wall his spine split into a dozen pieces. Melissa and Holly fired a bunch of spells before running for the now slowly moving Jeep.

One of the police officers suddenly woke to find himself lying on a mix of up-turned soil and fragmented flowers. As he got to his feet he couldn't believe his eyes. A blue Jeep full of women speeding away from a group of dark clothed ninjas. The girls looked like they were firing lightning and fire from their hands while the ninja people fired arrows and threw knives back at the girls. He wiped his eyes with the palm of his hands to make sure he wasn't imagining it and when he looked again the street was completely deserted.

The girls made sure they had lost their pursuers before they ditched the Jeep near the hospital. They removed the arrow before they took Alyson in. They were forced to lie through their teeth before handing her over. Melissa cast a few memory spells in order to remain inconspicuous. An hour in and there was no sign of the police or the would-be assassins. They were safe for now.

Holly and Nicole took the first watch on guarding duty. Meanwhile Helena, Melissa and Rachel went in search of some sugar. An upstairs Coca-Cola vending machine was greatly appreciated. Nobody had any money except Rachel so they depended on her to get the lot, she didn't mind. As Rachel handed over Helena's can of Fanta, Melissa could sense the chemistry in the air. She decided to use the opportunity to pop to the loo. The yellow and cream hallway was now empty except for Rachel and Helena. They glanced at one another awkwardly, like teenagers before their first snog. Rachel decided to make the first move, but Helena grabbed her so quick she didn't have the chance. They kissed with such a passion that they both cried. It lasted minutes but it felt like hours when Helena finally did pull away. It was a tinge of guilt that did it, she was still married after all.

CHAPTER 48

NIGHTSHINE

Rose and Anthony didn't like the corridor they were sent down. It was dark and dingy with wet patches on the floor. So they were relieved when they finally began heading towards a light source. Ryan was trying his best to catch them up and arrived in the same room seconds after them. They weren't surprised to see him, they heard his panting in the darkness. The room they had arrived in was grimy in appearance, but grand in scale. The ceiling must have been thirty-foot high. A decrepit monumental stair case led up to another level. Rose noticed the front desk and the dwarfish man sat at it. She approached him awkwardly.

"I am looking for somebody called Kayzor, am I in the right place?" She politely asked the man. Upon closer inspection, she noticed how awful he looked. His clothes were far too big for him and were lined with holes. He hadn't shaved in months, a thick fur covering most of his face.

"Wait!" Came a gruff response that sounded more like a bark than actual words. He signalled towards a set of seats before disappearing out the back somewhere.

While she waited Rose turned her attentions to the other stranger in the room. The middle-aged black man that had followed her and Anthony into the room.

"Hi. I'm Rose." She started before offering her hand.

"Ryan."

His handshake was strong, she liked that in a man. As they shook hands she thought that he looked familiar, but she couldn't work out where from. She dismissed it for the time being.

"I'm Anthony." Anthony quickly inserted as if to remind the pair of his presence in the room. He didn't bother shaking hands.

"Head for the door on the right." A gruff voice sounded. It was the dwarfish receptionist. Rose was surprised she didn't smell him entering because she could smell him now.

The trio had looked around the room upon their entry but none of them had noticed the three doors with huge white symbols painted on them, it was as if they were invisible until they were pointed out.

The door to the left was marked with a picture of a sun.

The middle door had a big star painted on it.

The door to the right was marked with a picture of a moon.

Anthony took a deep breath and walked through the door pretending he wasn't terrified of what stood behind it. The other two cautiously followed him through and the trio temporarily found themselves in darkness again. The phones were straight out as they continued on. The smell of damp and wet dog protruded through their nostrils, the steady tap of dripping water rhythmed in the background. The three of them were relieved when they finally reached a door, albeit a huge metal one. Rose bashed it with the side of her hand to save her knuckles. It was answered with a quickness that was deliberate, they were expected.

The man that answered wore long purple robes and sported an elongated ginger beard that made him look like a cartoon magician, he led them into the room with a smile. The room was vast with a giant table sitting central in the room, the kind of table you only see in films and TV shows with enough space to sit thirty men. The robed man took a seat next to a woman, a woman that looked more like a man. She appeared to have stubble from the very little light the trio were offered. The man motioned them to take a seat opposite him, which they obliged.

"Hello. I am Kayzor of the Nightshine pack, I understand the priest sent you all?" Kayzor questioned.

"Yes." Rose and Ryan murmured.

"Good. We are so glad to have you here as part of our werewolf pack." The woman announced with a huge wide grin.

CHAPTER 49

CROWN PRINCE

Halfway through another great day of fight training with Torus and Chora, David was disappointed to be greeted by a blue flashing light, meeting time. The training was good to take his mind off all the worries he was having about his friend Anthony. It was nice to see everyone though and have another Cannibal Café Coffee. David listened as Doc and Celeste explained that the vamp barman that was killed at Ah-Pla was beheaded by a mystery woman in yellow. Apex (the Royal Vampire police) were as secretive as always and would offer no more information on the case. So, for now, case closed. Celeste meanwhile, had decided to sell Priveam and become a bone-fide member of the group, which she could do as a member of Libra.

Trigger and Paige, who were working together on the Helena Pearce case, had since learnt that Helena was fostered just after birth, but they couldn't find any trace any of her birth parents. The group was slightly worried about Ryan who hadn't been in touch for a couple of days but knew he could take care of himself. But David was more worried about his friend Anthony who he knew was probably with Ryan. If one of them was in trouble they both were.

The rest of the base had been preparing for the imminent arrival of the Crown Prince. David was glad he was coming, he knew the distraction would ease his worry, even if only temporary. After the meeting was over the entire base mucked together for a spring clean. They didn't even have time to change when suddenly an alarm began sounding.

Winwood bypassed the security and hopped into the escalator to bring the Crown Prince down. As the lift shut up and out of sight, the rest of the lined up either side of the corridor and waited nervously. They stood anxiously for what seemed like hours before the left came back down. Four people exited the lift, Winwood and a smartly-dressed young man were followed by two burly gentlemen dressed in black.

It was obvious which was one was the Prince. His face was one of youth, yet his eyes showed the tiredness of travel. Fifteen going on four hundred. His clothes, as bright as his painted smile, were made from the finest silk but the seams showed a worn disposition. His sword swung sheathed at his side, hovering just out of fingertips reach. It showed a readiness that was all too familiar, and with it, a lack of trust. He hadn't lived his life; he had been moulded through it. His dyed bleach-blonde-hair shone through the gaps of his weighted silver crown like the final remnants of his soul. Shining its mutiny through his incarcerated existence. His only sign of rebellion to his mother, and the throne he was set to inherit.

His march along the hallway had the elegance the group expected, he lived the show the group sub-consciously demanded. Directly behind him, too close for comfort, walked his bodyguards. Two members of the Royal Guard, dressed like bouncers, both equally well built. After walking the line of Libra's, he turned and bobbed a quick bow to the group. The group did the same in return but hovered, not one of them knowing how long one was supposed to stay down for.

"Please rise." The Prince said as he looked in amazement at the size of the base before looking back at the group. "So, how are you all?"

"We are good thankyou Crown Prince." Winwood replied as he approached.

"Theo will do." He insisted before offering his hand out for Winwood to shake.

Winwood obliged with pleasure, bowing his head while he shook it.

"Please enough of this stupid bowing. While I am under your protection. You must consider me equal." The crown prince demanded lifting up Winwood's head before taking a good luck at the rest of the Libra staff. He was happy with the pleasantries, but always saw himself as equal to others. If there was one lesson his father had drummed into him before his untimely death, it was that. Over the next few hours everyone got to know each other a bit. At first it was over food, then over alcohol and then over a guided tour. Before long Theobald Evermore wasn't the Crown Prince anymore, he was a friend, much to the disgust of his bouncers Flint and Ward.

CHAPTER 50

THE BOY WHO CRIED WEREWOLF

Anthony, Rose and Ryan were all in shock. Every single one of their jaws would have dropped if they weren't all propping them up to hide their shock. They were all disappointed too, not a single one of them raised a suspicion despite the pitfall signs that were now flashing through their heads. Nobody was more disappointed than Ryan was in himself. Having been told by Winwood to stay alert, he had clearly not done so. He was taken aback by his own lack of preparation, one that had put him in this position. He didn't even have any weapons on him bar a run-of-the-mill knife.

"Well, what can we do for you?" The woman reiterated. Her increased tone gave the impression she was getting angry.

"We were sent cos we need help taking care of some vampires." Rose quickly answered.

Ryan felt his temper rising as he took in Rose's words. At that moment part of him wanted to lash out, part of him wanted to walk away. The part of him that stayed, stayed for David and Winwood.

"And you?" The manly woman directly addressed Ryan.

"Same reason." Ryan lied.

"Well you have come to the right place if its vampires you want dead." Seethed Kayzor through gritted teeth. It was as if the word 'vampire' itself carried a dirtiness to it. Like a swear word that cut the very air it was said into.

"How will you help us, and what do you want in return?' Rose asked. She was smart enough to realise nothing came for free these days.

"We have a process. It will make you stronger than you could imagine. One which I can personally guarantee the next time you came up against a vamp, you will be grateful for." Kayzor replied through a smile.

"As for something in return, you are helping us getting rid of vermin. It's a mutually beneficial cause." The woman croaked with laughter.

The trio of humans stood glancing at one another in shock, not knowing what to do or say next. Kayzor then pulled out what looked like a small remote control and pressed a button. A light flashed on in the darkest corner of the room to reveal two big metal doors. Each one had something sprayed onto them like the doors they had seen earlier.

The left side door had a huge white circle on it. The door to the right was the same sized circle, only it was painted red. The red one definitely looked the more ominous.

"There are two doors. The door to your left will lead you to a process to become a werewolf and join our pack. That's where you will find your revenge on the vamps that have done you harm. The door to the right is an exit where you can leave this place. But be warned, once you pick a door and enter, your choice is made and your decision is final. There will be no turning back." Kayzor announced with solidarity.

The three of them approached the doors as if they were wild animals. Curious yet careful. Anthony was the first to speak.

"What should we do?" Anthony whispered to Rose. He wanted to leave, this whole experience made him feel uneasy, but he didn't want to tell her that. He was along for the ride now, wherever it took him.

"I think we should leave." Ryan insisted. He decided he would tell them the truth once they were out of here.

"Fine by me." Anthony announced as he followed Ryan through the door.

Anthony turned in the room and was surprised to see Rose still standing there, as if she was considering life as a werewolf.

"Follow me Rose. I can help you." Ryan urged.

Yet still she stood there still unsure.

"Rose come on." Anthony tried.

Rose wasn't budging anytime soon. Ryan saw no choice now. He needed to act.

"I know where David is, and I can take you to him. Just please come with me now." Ryan announced to Anthony.

Anthony almost broke into tears, he couldn't speak for choking. He gave Rose a pleading glance and that was enough. She couldn't do it. She couldn't not help Anthony. She walked through the door with solidarity but was surprised as it slammed shut behind her, once again leaving the trio in complete darkness.

CHAPTER 51

BEDTIME STORIES

Alyson awoke to the sound of girls quietly arguing. As she began to stir it quickly ceased to silence. She realised she was surrounded by girls but it took her a good couple of minutes to remember who they were and why she was lying in bed. Her sisters fussed her as she remembered the events from the night before with the assassins. However, it wasn't long until the first of the questions arrived.

"Who were they? The people that were trying to kill you?" Helena asked nicely but her voice bordering on demanding.

Alyson didn't have a chance to answer as two nurses walked in to check her vitals. When they finally disappeared out of earshot Alyson began speaking.

"The people that shot me belong to a group called the Stalkers. Their single purpose it to find and kill magick people, witches like us."

"Why?" Melissa asked furiously. She wanted to go after them.

"No idea why they started it, but I know they've been at it years. The Stalkers are the group that started the witch hunts. They are responsible for the deaths of hundreds of thousands of witches and warlocks across the world over the last few centuries."

"How comes I've never heard of them?" Holly asked curious as to why she had never come across any mention of them in any of the books she had read.

"They are a secret society who will gladly silence any man, woman or child just to keep their existence a secret." Alyson informed.

"Who are they, where do they come from?" Helena asked.

"I heard they are a bunch of specialist people headhunted from all over the world. They are recruited from places like the Hunter Academies and are warped into thinking we are all evil."

The room fell silent as the questions ran out. It was then that one of the nurses approached and asked if some of the girls didn't mind leaving. Helena and Rachel agreed to do the first shift so Holly, Margaret and Melissa all gave Alyson a hug then left.

"Do you think we can beat them, the Stalkers?" Helena asked as she took a seat by Alyson's bedside.

"No. There's hundreds of them. This time we were lucky. You had the element of surprise. Next time you come up against them that advantage will be gone. And, you will come up against them again, they're probably building a file on each of you as we speak." Alyson said before glancing over to Rachel, it was the first time she had a chance to properly take her face in. Upon inspection, it was clear she wasn't related, she looked far too different for that.

"Who is your girlfriend then?" Alyson asked with a smile.

At first Helena wanted to deny it, but a sideways glance at Rachel convinced her otherwise.

"Rachel." Helena confirmed with an embarrassed grin.

"And how'd you meet?" Alyson asked curiously. It felt strange taking an interest in her sister's life, a sister she had literally just met. It also felt nice, the first time she had ever felt like part of a family.

"It's a really long story." Helena blushed.

"Come on. It's not like I will be going anywhere soon." Alyson urged.

Helena had nothing better to do, so she began her story. She started the night that Elathan turned up at her house and explained every moment vividly and excitedly as Alyson and Rachel listened intently.

CHAPTER 52

SACRIFICES

Helena and Rachel went to the hospital cafeteria for some food while Holly and the rest took their watch with Alyson. After a much-needed break and some welcome hot food Helena and Rachel grabbed six coffees to take back to the ward. As they eventually got to her bedside they were surprised to find the girls were sitting in complete silence. It was almost like they were waiting for something. Helena and Rachel handed everyone a coffee and stood around the bed eager to hear what was happening. It was obvious when Alyson began speaking that she was explaining her life and the girls were waiting for Helena so she didn't miss it.

"I was fourteen when I began doing magick. At first it was love spells, luck chants, jinxes. Kid's stuff really. As I got older, I got more powerful. Then a few year ago, I heard about blood magick. I read somewhere that if you had magical ancestors you had this stuff in your veins that made you more powerful than other normal witches. The further your magical bloodline went back, the stronger you were. Naturally, I started doing some digging."

Alyson stopped her story as a nurse walked in for routine observational checks, she didn't look happy there was so many girls around the bed but she said nothing. The girls waited impatiently for her to leave and were grateful when she finally did. As soon as the nurse was out of earshot, Alyson continued.

"I looked for records of my parents for months, but I found absolutely nothing. I could only trace my history back so far then it was guess work, but then it occurred to me. All it really took was a memory spell. I practiced and practiced until I could go all the way back."

"You mean?" Melissa was the first to work out.

"Wait, what are we talking about here?" Holly questioned.

"Our birth." Alyson said with a grimace.

"You saw the birth too?" Helena asked.

"Yeah, you've seen it?" Alyson asked with surprise.

"A daemon called Elathan showed us." Holly informed.

"So anyway, obviously you know there was originally six of us." Alyson said with a forlorn look on her face.

"There still is." Margaret informed.

"What do you mean?" Alyson asked curiously.

"Me and Nicole, we share this body." Margaret confirmed.

"Wow. Well pleased to meet you Nicole." Alyson said enthusiastically.

A wink through Margaret's face was Nicole's way of saying 'hello'.

"That's great. But it still doesn't explain how you knew my name when you saw me earlier." Holly added curiously

"So yeah, once I knew of your existence I screened you..." Alyson answered.

The silence in the room told Alyson they needed more information.

"It's a magick spell, a bit like scrying. Every now and then I watched you, just for a minute to make sure you were all okay." Alyson informed.

"Why didn't you tell us you knew about us?" Helena queried with more anger in her voice than she meant to put there.

"Cos of the Stalkers. I didn't want to put any of you in harm's way. But now it's too late." Alyson finalised as some nurses came in with plates of hot food for all the patients. The girls left before they were asked to, but Holly and Margaret didn't leave the bench outside the ward.

*****

Helena, Rachel and Melissa decided to go for some fresh air, and more coffee. As they exited the ward and turned a corner they were surprised to find a man just standing there looking straight at them. He seemed to be waiting. He looked like he was in his fifties, with greying hair and wrinkles. He was dressed entirely in purple. Periwinkle trousers, periwinkle jacket, periwinkle tie, a mauve shirt and mulberry coloured shoes. As they approached him he smiled.

"Alyson, Holly, Margaret?" He pointed at each of them guessing incorrectly.

"No." Helena answered with intrigue, she was alert but open to listening. The air turned cold around her fingers as her fist filled with ice.

"Damn worth a guess...Anyway don't worry I am the daemon Eblis. I'm here, cos Elathan sent me." He informed with an authoritative finger. The sound of his words was slightly masked by the polo he was rattling around in his mouth. He obviously had no conversational etiquette.

"He's alive?" Rachel asked delightedly. She was hoping he hadn't sacrificed his life for her.

"Yes. Obviously, otherwise I wouldn't be here..." He mused as he pulled out a packet of polos from his pocket, he picked out five and put them all in his mouth. He didn't offer the girls any before he put the rest of the packet away.

"...Now, he'll be fine, but he hasn't got the energy to skip, so has sent me in his place."

The man went into his pockets to pull out two pieces of paper. He had a quick look at them to see which was which. He put the other back in his pocket.

"This is a list of people you need." He said offering it out to the girls. Melissa took the paper off him. She un-creased it and read it aloud.

"The tainted man, the changed villain, the withering woman...What is this?"

"Obviously it is the first three souls you need to get." The man said before going back into his pocket for more polo's.

"Wait, what do we need these for exactly?" Helena demanded.

"You didn't think you could open a Helldoor without a sacrifice, did you silly? If you want your mam back, you are gonna have to swallow some of that almighty pride of yours. Besides, it's not exactly virgins your sacrificing, is it?" Eblis sneered.

Helena wanted to smash his face in. Rachel thankfully noticed and grabbed her hand to try and calm her down. It was ice cold.

"By sacrifice you mean kill people." Helena spat out.

"Of course. Sacrifice is the act of giving up one important thing in exchange of another equally important thing. To get six souls out, you need to pay with six souls." The daemon informed.

"It's not happening." Helena snapped.

"Oh well see you around." Eblis said about to disappear.

"Wait." Melissa started to stop the daemon from leaving. "Let's just say out of curiosity that we agree. Who are they? What's all this tainted man crap?" Melissa asked.

"The tainted man is somebody who has committed to a life of good virtue but has somehow ended on the path towards suicide. Luck or a change of heart may have saved them, but they are now damned to Purgatory when they do finally pass. The changed villain is somebody with a life of bad virtue, who has risked their life to save another. They too are damned to Purgatory. The withering woman is somebody who has a good heart, but has made bad life choices and their health is deteriorating because of it. A form of slow suicide if you will. Again, damned to..."

"Purgatory." The three girls sarcastically finished.

"Now instead of letting them pass to Purgatory naturally, we are sending them to Hell, in exchange for six souls that currently reside in Hell, your mother included." Eblis informed.

The fact the daemon spoke with ridiculously large hand movements annoyed Helena, his patronising tone antagonised her more. But the fact Eblis spoke with polos clattering about his mouth frankly boiled her piss. So much so, that in the end she had to remove herself from the situation.

"Bit of a temper that one." Eblis said with a pointed finger as she disappeared around a corner quickly pursued by Rachel.

"She burns hot and cold. Now where do I find these people?" Melissa asked.

"They are all here in this very hospital. Here's the names…" He said handing over the other piece of paper from his pocket. "…Get them to Kayll Road library over the road from the main entrance and I will skip them to your factory."

He turned to walk away.

"When?" Melissa shouted after him.

"What?" He asked turning back around.

"When? When do you need these by?" Melissa asked waving the paper in the air to remind him.

"Today." He said before disappearing into thin air.

CHAPTER 53

INTO THE WOLF'S MOUTH

Ryan was the first to get out his mobile phone. The torch light on it was enough to reveal the small room they were in. It led to what looked like a circular tunnel that curved off to the right-hand side. He begrudged the fact his phone had no signal before leading the way ahead.

"Thank you." Anthony said holding Rose's hand for a couple of seconds.

"I couldn't not help, could I?" Rose smirked.

As the trio continued forward the need for the torch became less and less as they proceeded towards some light. Eventually they could see clear as day and followed the light into a small oval room. It took a few seconds for them to realise where they were. It was a jail cell. In a surge of panic Ryan ran ahead to try and move the bars that blocked their path, they would not budge. Rose desperately pulled at the cell door, that wouldn't move either. Anthony desperately looked around as if expecting to find a deliberate hole that they could continue through.

Ryan put the torch back on his mobile phone and sprinted back up the dark corridor they had just come from. A few kicks against the door at the other end, told him that wasn't going to budge either, they were stuck. He returned to find Anthony and Rose had both given in and dropped to the floor. Ryan fell to his knees, shocked at his own stupidity. That's when he noticed Kayzor standing beyond the iron bars with a wry smile across his face.

244

"You said this was an exit." Ryan snapped.

"You honestly thought we would just let you leave with the location of our base so you could run and tell your little hunter friends?" Kayzor asked before laughing at their stupidity.

"We aren't hunters." Ryan protested.

"It's not what the contents of your car tell us." Kayzor said with an authoritative grin.

Ryan didn't bother protesting. It was obvious his jig was up. Rose slowly reached towards the back of her pants for her gun. Anthony noticed her movement and grabbed her hand before she got there. He held it in place to avoid suspicion.

"What do you plan to do with us?" Anthony asked as a distraction.

"We haven't decided yet." Kayzor said before turning around and walking away.

Rose waited until Kayzor's heavy footsteps were out of earshot before she threw Anthony's hand away.

"I could have killed him. Why did you stop me?" Rose sulked turning her back to him.

"Cos he would be dead, but we would still be stuck in here." Anthony snapped back.

Rose knew he was right, but that didn't sully her tantrum.

"Normal bullets in there?" A dejected Ryan asked from the corner of the cell where he had slumped into.

"Yeah, why?" Rose asked intrigued.

"Then unless you're a crack shot and hit his heart or brain you probably wouldn't have killed him. Werewolves have accelerated healing so any shot that isn't fatal is a waste of a shot. At best, you'd have pissed him off, and we would now be dead." Ryan informed while looking towards the exit where Kayzor disappeared. It looked like he was forming a plan.

"How do you know all this? And who are you anyway?" Anthony shouted.

"I know because I have hunted his kind before. I work for a group that catches or kills his kind when they go rogue." Ryan informed without lifting his head from the floor.

"Well if you're such a bloody expert, how comes you ended up in here with us." Rose sulked kicking one of the bars that barricaded her in. It hurt, a lot. But it helped calm her down a little.

"I ended up here cos I was sent to follow you." Ryan answered.

Anthony and Rose were shocked silent. It stayed like that for a while. Before either of them had a chance to ask it, Ryan answered their question.

"I work for a vampire clan. The base, it's not that far from here, if we can get to it, we will be safe there. We have David with us."

Anthony wanted to scream in celebration, but then he thought about Rose.

"Have you heard of someone called Daisy?" Anthony asked.

Tears formed in Rose's eyes. She couldn't believe it was Anthony's first question. She respected him for it and she would remember that. Up to that moment she saw him as an understudy, now she saw him as an equal.

"Sorry. The name isn't familiar..." Ryan replied.

Rose felt her heart sink as the tears from her eyes splashed on the floor. She quickly covered them with her feet.

"...But the people I work with, we might be able to help you find her." Ryan announced.

Meanwhile, Kayzor stood in the hallway listening. A human wouldn't have been able to hear the conversation from that far away. But, Kayzor wasn't human. He had heard everything the trio had said since his exit.

CHAPTER 54

BAD BLOOD

David got a bit of a shock as Winwood woke him up. He knew it was earlier than usual because he still felt tired.

"Quickly get dressed and go to the meeting room." Winwood quickly informed before heading for the door.

"What's up?" David asked through squinted eyes.

"Somethings happened." Winwood said before disappearing outside.

When David heard Winwood knocking on the next door along, the Crown Prince's room, he knew whatever it was, it was serious. He began to worry it had something to do with Anthony as he made his way across to the meeting room, he didn't bother washing or changing he just wanted to know what had happened as soon as possible.

When he got to the meeting room he was surprised to find that Doc and Chora were already present. They were busy watching the television which was projected onto the whiteboard screen. David was about to speak when he realised what he was seeing, as everybody else filtered in, they too fell silent. The high spirits from the previous night had now been extinguished as everyone watched in earnest.

The television broadcast itself, looked similar to the ones David was used to as a human. Two smartly dressed people, one man, one woman sat at a desk reading from an autocue. The main headline was about an attack on a vampire base. David read the video-printer at the bottom of the screen.

'TRINITY BASE ATTACKED – 19 DEAD!' titled the screen in black bold letters with a yellow backdrop to emphasise the message. The newsreaders went onto to report that...

"...No group had yet claimed responsibility for the attack. 19 vampires believed to have been present at the base, at the time of the attack. 19 bodies found dead so far. It was thought no one at the base had survived the attack. Event believed to have happened between 3AM and 6AM..."

As the news went on, the newsreaders began repeating themselves and reporting rumours.

"It's werewolves if you ask me." Doc suddenly spoke up as the news went to a break.

"Shut ya racist mouth Doc." Chora said disapprovingly.

"Well it wouldn't be the first time, would it?" Doc snapped back.

"Just cos you drink doesn't make you an alcoholic." Chora snuffed back.

David wanted to stand up for Chora but he didn't want to argue with Doc. So, he just sat there awkward and silent. He was grateful when the others began filling the room.

"...And anyway you can't say anything about drink..." Doc began.

"Alright you two, chill." Trigger put-in to try and quieten the pair.

"He started it." Chora sulked.

"I'm surprised by you Doc, are you forgetting we are supposed to be impartial." Legitus added.

"I'm just offering my opinion is all, surely I'm entitled to it." Doc whinged.

"Alright. That's enough." Winwood finalised, turning off the television.

The whole group sat there quiet. Everybody had something they wanted to get off their chest but nobody dared to speak, nobody except Theobald Evermore, the Crown Prince.

"I was supposed to be there." He mumbled. "That's the base I am supposed to be at now." Theo reiterated.

"Then that means... your double?" Winwood questioned.

"Yes. And my scribe Yufalus." Theobald said.

Theobald looked pale, then white. Then pale white. Then he was sick all over the floor.

CHAPTER 55

SOUL SISTERS

The girls took a vote, had an argument, took another vote, and decided they had all come too far to stop now. Yet still, they each had to convince themselves that the people they were sacrificing somehow deserved it. They were the faceless detriments of society who warranted eternal damnation. A justifiable sacrifice, just this once. The girls drew lots for partnerships. It ended with Holly and Melissa as one pair, Alyson and Helena as another, leaving Rachel and Nicole as the final team.

After the girls teamed up with their partners they drew lots again, this time for which sacrifices they had to get. Holly drew the 'tainted man'. Nicole picked out the 'changed villain'. It was just Helena's luck that she was left with longest straw, the 'withering woman', the one that she wanted the least. After convincing the nurses to let Alyson go out for lunch, albeit with a little magick, they grabbed a wheelchair and Helena wheeled her out of the ward. As the girls arrived at the hospital lifts, the three groups all went their separate ways, each to their own missions. Helena and Alyson had to head for Ward E42.

They were both surprised to find how easy it was to get about with Alyson in a wheelchair and dressed in hospital robes. Nobody had given them a second glance. A nurse even offered to hold the door for them as they arrived at the ward entrance. They were in. A quick glance at a whiteboard told them where Victoria Daniels was. They headed to the private ward slowly but surely. A steady pace ensured no direct suspicion. As soon as they got in the room Helena closed the door behind them. Alyson got out of the wheelchair and headed towards one end of the patient, while Helena went to the other end.

Helena felt sick and her heart raced as she glanced to the bed. Lying there was a frail yet young-looking woman, her bald head evidence of her recent rigorous chemotherapy. The lack of make-up was evidence of her losing battle. She was dying. The visual revelation didn't help Helena feel any better about what she was about to do and acrimonious guilt ripped through the pair of them as they carefully lifted the frail woman from the bed to the wheelchair. Tears streamed down both of their faces as the woman put up the little fight that she still had left. As she took in their faces a glimmer of hope shone through. She wanted death and hoped they would be the ones to bring it. She was tired from the fight and was done with the land of the living. The girls wiped their faces and headed out with their heads down.

They made it over to Kayll Road library without being stopped. Both of them were pleased to find it empty other than Eblis who was impatiently waiting for them. He was irritably chewing aloud again, but they concentrated on the job at hand and wheeled the wheelchair towards him. Suddenly they found themselves in the factory again. The familiarity of their base a welcome repose for Helena. It was all new to Alyson.

The girls wheeled the woman into a big chamber that wasn't there previously, she wasn't alone. Nobody wanted to admit it but everybody felt guilty and wanted to stop. Nevertheless, three bodies were now in the chamber, three souls ready for sacrifice. Before they had a chance to moan about what they were doing. Eblis handed out another piece of paper to Alyson.

"The solid spirit... What does that mean?" Alyson asked.

"It's someone that's stuck in this world, that was meant to have passed onto another plain. Basically, someone or something that doesn't belong here." Eblis answered between blowing bubbles with his chewing-gum and popping them.

"Like a ghost?" Melissa queried.

"Exactly." Eblis said before blowing up and popping his gum bubble once more.

"I think I know where we might find one, but I have no idea how to catch one." Melissa informed.

"I think I do." Alyson answered.

Eblis and the girls were glad Alyson did, because nobody else had a clue. Eblis grabbed them both by the hand and they all disappeared. Seconds later he reappeared without them. He momentarily seemed to forget the whole reason he was there before his brain clicked and from his pocket he removed another piece of paper. Helena was tempted to go for it but something held her back. Instead Holly walked over and took it from him. She read it to herself a couple of times attempting to make sense of it before giving in and reading it aloud.

"The eternal sleeper!?"

"Someone who is neither dead nor alive. Obviously, somebody in a coma." Eblis said as if it was the most obvious thing in the world.

"You coming?" Holly uttered in Nicole's direction before walking towards Eblis.

"Sure." Nicole answered as she walked over to Eblis and Holly. The second she got there the three of them disappeared into thin air.

"Guess it's us two then." Rachel said with a smile walking over towards Helena grabbing her hand. Helena pulled her in for a quick kiss. A kiss that was interrupted by the sound of a chewing-gum bubble pop.

"Sorry girls. We have work to do." Eblis said before handing over his final piece of paper. Rachel took it and read it aloud.

"The sole survivor..." Rachel said motioning for an explanation.

"Somebody that should have died but didn't." Eblis informed.

The girls silence showed they needed more to work with than that.

"Someone that survived something that should have killed them. Like the only survivor of a bus crash or something." Eblis enlightened.

The girls continued their look of puzzlement.

"Don't worry, I know just the girl." Eblis said as he took both their hands and they disappeared.

CHAPTER 56

A DOGS DINNER

It was their first day of captivity and the first thing the werewolves did was search Rose's and Ryan's cars. The interiors were completely stripped. Weapons, fuel, upholstery, engine and all. On their second day, they were suddenly grabbed and searched by men three times their size, robbing them all of their mobiles and the little arsenal and hope that they had left. By the fourth day they were all so hungry they had no choice but to eat the mush that they were being served. All three of them tried to imagine something else as they wolfed down what they suspected to be the contents of three tins of dog food. On their sixth day, somebody new brought them their food, and it was accompanied by a chocolate bar each.

"What's the catch?" Ryan asked as he grabbed his food and inspected the chocolate bar with suspicion.

"Shhh." The woman whispered as she handed over their food.

The trio looked up from their grub to inspect the woman that had brought it in. Her face was kind with barely any stubble. She looked unlike every other werewolf they had seen to date, she almost looked human. Athletic and muscular, but human nonetheless.

On the eighth day, they were pleased to see her return. This time she had sneaked in a loaf of bread and cans of pop to go with their drool.

"Thankyou. Who are you?" Rose asked.

"My name is Kyrie. My friends mean to kill you, but I will get you out." She whispered before disappearing into the shadows leaving the group with more questions than they had food.

On the tenth day Kyrie returned. She had no treats this time but she did have some good news. She had managed to sneak a couple of weapons out of the armoury and would bring them on the night they all escaped together. Ryan promised her sanctuary at the Libra base if she helped them with their prison break. It was an agonising five days later when Kyrie finally knocked out the guard and took the keys off his unconscious body. She released the trio, handed over their weapons (two guns and a metal pipe) and so it began. The escape to Libra base.

The foursome managed to get halfway out of the base before they were even confronted. Two meagre-looking patrol men were quickly dispatched by Kyrie and Ryan who choked them both unconscious. They tip-toed unnoticed through another few corridors and hallways and were almost out, when the alarm finally sounded. It barked above them like a thousand dogs. It was deafening. Ryan wedged his metal pipe underneath the doorframe to stop them being followed and they continued on. As they headed towards the final door they found their path suddenly blocked. They all backed away with worry as the two human shapes transformed into two behemoth-looking werewolves. Skin turning from black to blue, nose stretching out into a snout, teeth growing to fang. They growled their anger and barked their dominance before they ran on all fours at the group.

Anthony remembered his gun and pulled it out firing all six rounds into one of the wolves. It clearly hurt as the wolf snarled, but it looked more pissed-off than injured. But it was enough of a distraction for Kyrie, who had transformed into her wolf-form without any of the others noticing. She knocked the distracted wolf down the hallway like a bowling ball, landing with a thud.

Her successful attack left her exposed and the other wolf pounced on her, biting her neck and shoulder before Kyrie circled and threw it off. Anthony, Ryan and Rose stood helpless as the wedged doors behind them began rattling and moving. They saw no choice but to make a run for it. In the middle of the corridor Kyrie and the wolf took turns lunging at each other trying to lock a well-gripped bite around each other's neck. The trio ran for it and managed to speed through the middle of the stare-down and towards the exit. However, at the end of the corridor they found themselves face to face with the other werewolf that was back on its paws, he was bearing his fangs in delicious excitement. He growled and barked his anger then ran straight at them. The trio screamed and ran towards the werewolf, who was surprised as he was stampeded backwards through the door.

They turned to see Kyrie limping towards them. Her front left leg clearly bitten. Behind her lay the corpse of the werewolf she was fighting, neck ripped out, a testament to Kyrie's strength. They slammed the door shut behind her as she emerged from the building. They wedged the door in place with a nearby stick before they all ran towards Ryan's car. Kyrie was forced to transform into her human form so she didn't slow them down. Anthony didn't feel well all of a sudden, but he was determined to keep going. Ryan's jaw dropped as he noticed upon closer inspection that most of his car and its contents were missing. A quick check under the bonnet confirmed his suspicions, even the engine was gone.

CHAPTER 57

THE GIRL IN YELLOW

Over half the Libra clan had left the base for different missions but David was pleased to learn a few people, including him and Chora were staying behind. Things had been awkward between them since the asylum and some fight training was the perfect way to spend some time together without the awkwardness of forced conversation. David, Trigger, Doc, Chora and the Crown Prince Theo started with the basics, before eventually moving onto full sparring before dinner. It was nice for David who finally won a spar, besting both an unfit Doc and an untrained Theo. But he still wasn't quite a match for Trigger or Chora.

After dinner David was excited to learn that they were finally using Pulse guns. Trigger explained that the guns were just glorified BB guns with electrically charged bullets. One single bullet was equivalent to a really powerful taser and would knock out most humans, vamps and werewolves. They all took turns firing the Pulse guns at a range of different targets. They started with giant targets which gradually got smaller before they eventually moved onto moving targets. It was quite fun to watch the lighting bullets fizzle upon contact and David was a natural. He was slightly better than Chora, who clearly wasn't pleased about it. It was probably due to the amount of time he had spent playing videogames as a human.

David took a seat and reflected on his life as Theo and Doc took their turn firing the guns. He was unrecognisable from the weedy teen that first came to the base months earlier. His hair was now permanently shaved short, his body had developed into a mass of muscle and his confidence carried him elegantly. He was a colossal of his former self.

*****

Winwood, Legitus and Torus found themselves in an abandoned house. It was once a great mansion complete with a swimming pool and marble floors. Now it reeked of damp and putrid wood and contained the remnants of many teenage drinking sessions. The vampires didn't need an enhanced sense of smell to pick up the many half-bottles of cider that littered the place. They eagerly awaited Cerevad who had phoned them pleading for their protection. The only reason Winwood agreed to help was so he could get some information on Legion, the illegal research company that Cerevad worked for. The trio set up a few traps and waited patiently in the darkness barely sharing a word.

It was a welcome relief when Cerevad did finally show, a whole forty-seven minutes later than he said he would. He had hoped Winwood wouldn't turn up alone and was pleased to smell the evidence of two others hidden in the shadows. What he didn't know was that Legitus and Torus already had their guns pointed and were ordered to shoot if he so much as moved.

"Winwood. It is good to see you." Cerevad announced himself with a humorous smile.

There was no doubt it was him. He was a celebrity in the criminal world and he carried the persona to match. Every law enforcement agency in the country had pursued him at some point, the Libra clan included. His face had been plastered across hundreds of wanted posters over the last two decades, each of them carrying the wisenheimer smile that he was currently wearing.

"Cerevad. We finally meet." Winwood smouldered.

"I wasn't sure if you would show." Cerevad offered.

"The same applies to you. Now, to business." Winwood skipped.

"Ever so quick to pass up the pleasantries aren't we." Cerevad noted before pausing, he seemed to be on edge, like he was listening for something. Legitus and Torus tightened their grips around their guns and edged their fingers towards their triggers.

"What do you want?" Winwood asked.

"There is a woman who is after me. I need her taken out of the equation."

"If it was just a woman, you wouldn't need us." Winwood said with a smile. He wasn't stupid.

"This girl has a special talent for killing." Cerevad retaliated.

"Who is she? Why does she want you dead?"

"She was Legion, now she isn't." Cerevad simplified.

"I want your boss." Winwood tried.

"I don't know where he is." Cerevad said quickly as if he had already anticipated the question.

Winwood turned his back to walk away. Cerevad wasn't ready for that.

"I will tell you where the research base is."

Winwood waited. He needed more to convince him to stay.

"It's on the west coast."

Winwood took another step towards the door.

"It's in a town called Hollyby. Just up from Maryport. I can take you there." Cerevad pleaded. Whatever had spooked him clearly wasn't letting up its chase.

"You have to give me something more. Something else Cerevad." Winwood said turning around to face him.

"Fine. David Sixsmith, I know who sired him."

The shot was like a punch in the gut, Winwood had no choice but to listen.

"How could you know that?" Winwood asked. He was suspicious, yet curious.

Legitus and Torus were also curious, their fingers eased from the triggers but their guns remained pointed at their mark.

"My boss wanted him because of his sire. I dinno how they know, I'm not part of the research team, but we brainwashed his parents ready to lure him to us."

"So why didn't you take him?" Winwood urged.

"Well we found out he had joined you lot, so we took over Priveam in a ploy to found out where your base was and get him back."

"That's why you had Celeste at the bar." Winwood fumed. "You were gonna lure one of us there for a trade." Winwood was now shouting, his voice echoed throughout the empty mansion.

"Yes, but some stupid humans turned up and distracted us. And then your whole gang turned up. I couldn't put up a fight against your lot with a bunch of newbies." Cerevad whinged.

"You'd literally just turned them vamps, that's how they died when they were shot with the lightning bullets." Winwood guessed. "By the way, my order still stands." He reaffirmed to Legitus and Torus who had since lowered their guns. They aimed again.

The delay was distraction enough for Cerevad who suddenly ran forwards. Four shots were fired, all behind Cerevad. Three of the lightning bullets fizzled into the chest of a woman who had suddenly burst through the window at his rear. This was Cerevad's plan all along, he was just waiting for the right moment. He knew he was being followed and knew Winwood would turn up guns blazing. The woman who attempted to prop herself up with what looked like a sword for a forearm, was dressed entirely in yellow. She struggled to maintain her balance before she ultimately fell to the floor dazed.

Cerevad quickly ran back over to the other side of the room wrapping his sweaty hands around her neck strangling her. She didn't have the strength to retaliate and her life began to ebb away. As the colour began to drain from the woman's face Cerevad felt a blow to the back of his head, his grip loosened before he fell unconscious to the floor next to the brick that felled him.

CHAPTER 58

THE SURVIVOR

It took Helena and Rachel hours to find anything. They had been forced to look through old newspaper cuttings in a library, but eventually they found what they were looking for. There was a woman called Kate who had tried to kill herself by jumping from a bridge. Helena recognised the photo but put it down to the fact she had probably seen the story on the news or read it in the paper at the time. The article mentioned it was a hotspot for suicides and Kate was believed to have been the first one to ever survive the fall. After convincing a female librarian that they were journalists she gave them an address.

Helena and Rachel hopped in a taxi and went straight there. It turned out she didn't live there anymore, but thankfully a neighbour had stayed in touch. He was more than happy to pass on Kate's new address to the girls. After all they were roughly the same age, and he had no reason to suspect they meant her harm. As they visited the new address they were again disappointed. It turned out that it was Kate's parent's home and that she had her own flat now. Posing as old-school friends, the girls convinced Kate's parents to hand over her current address and soon after they found themselves face to face with Kate's front door. Helena did the knocking.

"Please, please, please." Rachel joked with fingers crossed.

Helena's smile soon turned to shock as she found herself opposite a half-naked man. As she moved her eyes slowly up his sweaty body to his face she was dumbstruck to see who it was.

"Helena?" He said in awe. It was her husband Tom.

Helena turned on heel marching away, every step was a fight against the urge she had to stay. The lust and love she had for her husband, feelings she thought she was over. The rage she had for Kate, Helena now realised why she recognised the picture in the newspaper. Kate was the bitch that was posing as 'Steve', the woman who was having an affair with her husband. Tom quickly put on trousers and trainers and was out of the door after her. He wanted an explanation, but a small part of him genuinely missed her.

Rachel didn't understand what was going on, but she had guessed. She walked through the open door into the house and closed the door behind her. Kate had since dressed and came into the room to see what was going on. She found herself face to face with Rachel. She didn't have a chance to speak before Rachel sent her across the room and into a wall, then another, then another and another. It wasn't long before everything in the house was broken including Kate's arm, collar bone, her wrist and four of her fingers.

Tom had caught up to Helena and pulled on her shoulder to turn her round. He didn't expect to be sent across the car park through the air. He looked confused, he looked scared. He looked around for some explanation of what had just happened.

"Why? Why did you do it?" Helena said marching towards him as sirens began to sound in the background. Rachel's violent streak had prompted a neighbour to call the police. Rachel noticed the noise and marched Kate outside. Half of the neighbours peeped out to see Rachel pulling her along the corridor. One of them tried to stop her, they then found themselves suddenly contending with a fire inside their home instead.

Tom was backing away from Helena, he didn't understand who she was anymore, or what. Helena laughed as he retreated away petrified. His feeble backing away soon became a run as she neared him. Helena stopped him and fired him through the air and into a set of nearby metal bins. His shoulder cracked with the force.

"Answer my question." Helena demanded.

"Please. I'm sorry. It was a mistake." Tom pleaded. He didn't bother trying to escape again he just lay there pathetically begging for his life, like a little girl. Helena laughed at his feeble request for mercy.

"I know it was a fucking mistake. I want to know why you did it?" Helena demanded. Embers rained from the gaps in her fists. Tom began to shiver with fear.

"Please." He tried backing further into the bin shed.

"Why." Helena repeated.

There was a pause as Tom considered his options. All of one them.

"Cos... Cos I was bored." He cried through a face full of tears. He was scared for his life and sobbing like a baby. Helena had never been less attracted to anybody in her life. She was over him.

"Thankyou. That wasn't so hard was it." Helena sneered before generating a giant fireball with both of her hands. Luckily for Tom, Elathan had turned up just in the nick of time skipping Helena out of there. The fire ball that she fired was like a bright red meteor. The sisters were impressed as it burned right through the factory wall smouldering to ash in the field outside.

CHAPTER 59

FACTORY GIRLS

Rachel made her way down the steps to where Helena was. A quick glance up and down the street told her there was no sign of Helena at all. Rachels worry turned to fear as three police cars and a police van came skidding to a halt right in front of her. A bunch of officers surrounded her and began closing in. She wasn't sure what would be worse, going to jail or being sent back to the asylum. There was too many of them to resist, even magick wouldn't get her out of this one.

Rachel let go of Kate and fell to her knees worrying about her fate. It was then that the police were suddenly blinded by a flash of white light. When they could see again there was no sign of Rachel, or her hostage. Eblis had skipped them both to the factory. As he marched Kate straight for the sacrifice chamber Holly had to stop Helena from killing her. Rachel was far too dumbstruck and half-blinded to figure out what was happening. She was pleased when her eyes eventually focused on the factory wall and she could hear Helena cursing.

As Eblis put the sobbing woman in the chamber, Helena stormed off to see Rachel. She moved in to give her a tight hug, a hug which turned into a snog. Helena kissed Rachel with such a passion and admiration that she had never kissed Tom with before. A fake cough from Holly finally parted their mouths. Everyone approved of the newly-formed relationship between the pair, but there was a time and place for such things, and it wasn't now. The girls had a spell to finish.

*****

The commotion the girls had caused in the last couple of days had alerted several of Winwood's sources of their presence. Paige and Celeste were forced to go through piles and piles of evidence. After days of going through police reports, CCTV and witness statements the two vamps had six names. Holly Hamilton, Alyson Quinn, Helena Pearce, Melissa Jones, Margaret Reed and Rachel Grey. Twenty-four hours later they had a recent location and found themselves getting out of a taxi into a quiet street. The taxi driver pointed up the hill towards an empty looking factory.

"That wer' it." He declared before collecting his money and driving off.

They didn't believe him and decided to check it out for themselves. Paige removed a camera from her bag while Celeste opted for a EMF which spiked full-red as they approached the factory. A quick search around the building resulted in nothing so they began to look for a way in. A sneak peek through a hole in wall told them nobody was home, but they noticed a giant chamber that took up a large chunk of the factory.

"What is that?" Celeste questioned while Paige took a look."

"...I think it's a sacrifice chamber." Paige gulped.

"For sacrificing what?"

"People. We have to tell Winwood before it gets used." Paige informed before removing her camera to take some photographs of the factory and its surrounds.

Ten minutes later Paige and Celeste had the place scoped out and were heading back to Libra base to tell Winwood what they had found.

CHAPTER 60

RUN, FOREST, RUN

With no form of transport in sight Kyrie, Ryan, Rose and Anthony had no choice but to make a run for it. They sped off into a darkened field with worry they wouldn't make it. Ryan and Rose struggled to keep up with the relentless pace Kyrie was setting. But Anthony struggled to stay in touch with the two humans who lagged behind. As the howls around them neared they knew they didn't have long before they were caught.

"How long have we got?" Ryan questioned as they stopped for a few seconds to allow Anthony to catch up.

"Not long. But I might have an idea." Kyrie suggested. "This way." She said diverting their route from the green fields they were currently running in, to a nearby council estate.

"Why here?" Ryan asked, as he and Kyrie helped Anthony and Rose climb a metal fence into the empty street.

"I'm hoping they have to change into human form here. That will give us a level playing field while Anthony catches his breath." Kyrie hoped.

"What's up, are you okay?" Rose asked Anthony as they stood waiting for the others to climb the fence.

"Nothing I'm fine." Anthony snapped.

The truth was he didn't know what was wrong with him. Only that he didn't feel right and was struggling to keep up with the others. He tried to think of a reason he felt so unfit but none come to mind. Kyrie and Ryan climbed over the fence and they all began running again. It was less than five minutes later when the werewolves arrived at the same street. As Kyrie predicted they stopped on the edge of town angrily barking and howling before switching to their less scary human forms. However, they still had the same keen sense of smell and could therefore still follow the scent that the escapees were leaving behind.

Anthony felt like they were running around in circles, little did he realise it was deliberate. As they headed into a small housing estate Anthony had a chance to catch his breath.

"Everybody wait here!" Ryan demanded before disappearing towards a block of flats.

It felt like he was gone for minutes and they were all relieved when he came running back with handfuls of stuff. Due to the darkened street, it was until he was right up close that any of them realised what he had in his hands. Clothes.

"Strip off and put these on." Ryan demanded as he handed over piles of clothes to everyone.

Thankfully Ryan didn't have to explain this unusual and prompt request. Everybody got it and quickly did what he said.

"Kyrie, can you disperse these and track us to catch back up?" Ryan questioned as he pulled all the old clothes together.

"Yes." Kyrie said before grabbing Anthony and having a good whiff of him.

Rose didn't expect to feel the tinge of jealously that suddenly surged through her as she watched Kyrie sniff Anthony. It dissipated as Kyrie disappeared around the corner with all the unwanted clothes that they were all just wearing. Rose, Anthony and Ryan set off again, running in the opposite direction.

"I think there is a hunter's outpost not too far from here, we just have to make it there and we should be able to hold them off until my friends come to help us." Ryan panted.

It was a whole eighteen minutes later before the werewolves realised what the group had done. Kayzor had worked it out as several of his pack returned with random items of clothing.

"You know what Kyrie smells like, focus on her." Kayzor growled to his pack. They all took a series of sharp inhales before heading off after her.

The distraction gave Ryan and the others enough time to get to the safehouse that he had mentioned. It was a hunter's building disguised as an old church. He went in alone at first. When he returned he had in his hand what appeared to be an old worn-woollen blanket. He wrapped it around Kyrie and guided her carefully into the safe house. Anthony and Rose followed with looks of confusion. Once inside Ryan closed the doors behind them and offered an explanation.

"The entrances and walls are warded preventing an array of creatures from entering, werewolves included…"

Ryan proceeded to light a dozen candles in the room. The inside looked decrepit but it was intact.

"…The blanket blocks the sigils and allows you to enter." Ryan finished.

"How does it work?" Kyrie questioned worryingly.

"The magick in it is beyond my comprehension I am afraid. You can take it off now if you want."

Kyrie carefully removed the blanket from around her waist. She looked scared, as if she could burst in to flames at any moment. Anthony tried his best to prop himself up on a table while Ryan searched the building. He returned with far less than anybody expected him to. A half-empty first aid box and a gun was all that he could find. Although it had six bullets in the barrel, there wasn't enough for the number of wolves they had in pursuit. After another frantic search, this time in more and more desperately abstract locations Ryan returned with nothing again. This time he couldn't hide the anger.

"The lazy..." Ryan seethed with a boot directed at one of the pews. He was surprised the entire back support of the long chair broke completely and fell to the floor with an echoing thud.

Anthony was struggling to stay upright. He was tired and cold and felt like he was going to collapse. Then he did collapse. When he came back around he realised he was on his back on the cold hard floor of the church. Rose was on one side holding his hand, with Ryan on the other side checking his body. Kyrie was stood above them looking over. Ryan stopped his search when he found what he was looking for.

"He's been bit. If you don't get him to the Libra base quick he will..." Ryan said as Anthony opened his eyes.

"I'll what?" Anthony lamely joked.

It was then that Anthony noticed the howling noises that were coming from around the church. They sounded far too close. He knew it was too late and they had been caught.

CHAPTER 61

STORM

Paige and Celeste finally made it back to the Libra base just as a thunderstorm began sounding overhead. The thunder, lightning and stotting rain was no longer visible once they took the lift underground. Celeste went straight to Winwood's office to tell him the news, while Paige hurried to the library. By the time Winwood was ushered to the library Paige already had the book out that she needed to show him. It was spread out on the desk, contents showing. As Winwood approached she pointed at a specific part of the book, he read the text aloud to save an intrigued Celeste the trouble.

"The six souls is a dark magick spell that allows you to swap souls between different realms. To get six souls out of a realm such as Purgatory or Hell you must trade-in six specific souls in return. These are typically known as the changed villain, the eternal sleeper, the sole survivor, the solid spirit, the tainted man and the withering woman. Although there are variations of these sacrifices, these listed are the most common. This spell can only be completed by six witches whom are related, and whom must also make their own sacrifices in order to complete the spell." Winwood said still looking rather puzzled.

"So, who are these witches exactly?" He asked.

Paige ran over to get some pieces of paper that had been printing-off on the other side of the room. She placed the first sheet down on the desk for Winwood, he recognised her straight away.

"Helena." Winwood pointed out.

"Yes. Throw in Rachel Grey and Margaret Reed, two of the three escapees from Shorebank psychiatric hospital, Helena must have been the third." Paige informed as two more pieces of paper went onto the table.

Three more similar-looking faces went down on the table, one after another, like badly printed mugshots.

"Holly Hamilton. Alyson Quinn. Melissa Jones. I think this makes up the six." Paige finalised.

"Ok. What your saying is. These six are witches are planning on sacrificing six people to get six people from Hell?" Winwood simplified.

"Well it could be from purgatory, limbo, paradise, even Heaven but yeah." Paige corrected.

"How are these related though?" Winwood asked.

"They are all the same age, so I'd guess they're sisters. I'm guessing they all went into care as babies and got separated. I can't find anything on their parents but I'm guessing that's two people they want out of wherever they are breaking people from." Paige finalised.

"Ok we have to stop them. What do you suggest?" Winwood asked.

"They are human so one lightning bullet should do it." Paige reasoned.

"Ready everything tonight, we storm the factory first thing in the morning." Winwood commanded.

*****

Winwood called a meeting and told the other vamps what was happening. At first light, most of them would be setting off to try and stop the coven of witches from completing the spell. Torus and Celeste were staying behind to look after the Crown Prince, but everybody else was going on this dangerous mission.

Winwood would have liked Ryan to come on the mission, but he didn't know where he was. He had barely texted the last couple of weeks, which was so unlike him. But over the last few days the updates had completely dried up and Winwood was worried to say the least. There was no-one he would rather have by his side going into battle, than his best friend Ryan.

CHAPTER 62

FINAL PREPARATIONS

It was the night before the spell and the girls were all perched around the bubbling cauldron with alcohol in their hands. Holly kept glancing at the time as it neared 11 o clock. In her fist was a set of final instructions from Elathan. She hadn't read it yet, but she knew he was going to ask for something big from the girls who had already given up so much. She got up from the cold factory floor and coughed to clear her throat. Everyone quietened as she opened up the piece of paper and read it aloud.

"Dear girls. It's me, your mother..." She struggled to breath as the words dawned on her. The others sat silently with open mouths and teary eyes.

"...Well done on getting so far, but there is a little bit more needed to get us over the finish line..." Holly said struggling to hold herself together. Helena got up, walked over and put her arm around her sister. Holly took a deep breath and continued.

"...I know you have already sacrificed so much to get us here. But in order to complete the spell you must sacrifice more. I hate to ask this of you but it is the only way..." Holly stopped to catch her breath before finishing the note. "...To finish the spell, you must all sacrifice an item which you hold most dear. If you have to question it. That's not it."

Holly turned the note over in the hope there was more information. There wasn't.

"What do you think it means." Rachel asked unsure if she was included.

"We must all give up our favourite possessions." Alyson suggested.

It took the girls a bit time to think, then one by one the girls moved around the cauldron ready to give up their favourite things forever. Helena glanced down at her wedding ring which glimmered its solidarity around her finger, willing her to change her mind. Although it reminded her of her lying, cheating excuse of a husband, it was also a memento of her favourite moments. She took it off, hovered and then dropped it into the green bubbling liquid regretting her choice the instance it left her fingers.

Holly went into her pocket and removed a beaten old house key for a door that didn't exist anymore, her childhood home. As a kid, it was a gift from her foster parents, one to remind her that whatever happened she would always be welcome in their home, even if she didn't live there anymore. But to Holly it wasn't just a house key. It was acceptance and love. It was the friendships she had forged as she was growing up, it was the family she had inherited. It was her entire childhood manifest into an item in the form of a key. Holly didn't want to but she let it drop from the palm of her hand into the bubbling liquid.

Margaret and Nicole had only one material possession. It was an old 2p piece that reminded each of them of their shared duality. If Margaret was the head of the coin, then Nicole would no doubt be its tail side. Alyson was forced to give up her rabbit's foot necklace. It had been her lucky charm since she was a kid and she genuinely believed it had kept her alive up to that point. She was clearly gutted to be giving it up. Melissa put in her biker jacket. It was the very same jacket she wore when she lost her virginity, rode her first motorbike, did her first magick spell. It had been with her for as long as she could remember and she was still making memories with it. It was like a second skin and she felt naked without it as put it into the cauldron.

The liquid bubbled like foam and changed colour from bright green to red, to violet, to blue, to black and then back to bright green again. The girls were unsure if that was supposed to happen, but they were pleased that the items they had lost had some effect at least. Feeling a little depressed about losing their favourite things the girls decided to have a drink and drown their sorrows. So, until the early hours of the morning the girls sat around the cauldron sharing booze, stories and the occasional secret before they all eventually went to bed.

*****

At six o clock in the morning Helena could no longer ignore the butterflies or the nervousness in her tummy, so she got up. She was surprised to find Rachel was already up and was busy making sure the CCTV they had installed together was working properly, which it was. If anybody came to try and stop them today, they would know about it.

CHAPTER 63

WERECAT AND MOUSE

Ryan was now pacing the room, desperately thinking of what he could do to get out of the situation. He stopped as something occurred to him and he ran over to the first aid box. He began scouring through the contents of the box again with desperate hope. The disappointment on his face showed he didn't find what he was looking for but he did find something he could use. It was an orange pill that he popped into his mouth and began chewing before anybody else in the room could question it.

"What was that?" Kyrie queried.

"Diazepam, to help with the nerves." He explained to the disapproving glances he was getting from her and Rose.

Rose knew what Diazepam looked like, and therefore knew he was lying. Despite this she still trusted Ryan, and whatever he was up to. Anthony let out a groan of pain as if to remind the others of his presence. He was white and clammy and seemed to be in a lot of agony. Even Rose, who knew nothing of his symptoms, could see he wouldn't last much longer.

"When did this even happen?" Rose sulked as she held Anthony's hand, he was cold to the touch.

"It must have happened in the escape." Ryan said taking Anthony's pulse.

"Why didn't he tell me." Rose questioned.

"We were a little preoccupied and he probably didn't want to slow us down." Ryan sympathised.

Meanwhile, the werewolves were outside still trying to find a way in. They had felt the sting of magick from the walls and had tried getting in through the roof with no luck. But now Ryan could hear them tunnelling below the church. He wasn't even sure if they could get in from below, as far as he was aware nobody had ever thought of the idea and he doubted the floor was warded. Either way, he knew they didn't have long before the werewolves found a way in.

"There's a hidden exit in the confession box. Rose, do you know where Penshaw monument is?" Ryan questioned as he readied his gun.

"Yeah of course." Rose assured.

"The Libra vampire base is underneath it. There's a big woodland at the back of it. That's where you'll find the entrance."

"What if we can't find it?" Kyrie worried.

"Then hopefully my friends will find you…" Ryan said before lifting Anthony's body from the table and carrying him over to Kyrie. "…You will have to carry him. Follow Rose. Don't worry, you'll be safe if you give them my name."

"You aren't coming with us, are you?" Rose asked.

By now, the sound of digging was coming from directly underneath them. They could feel the vibrations of each paw stroke.

"I will delay them, give you a fighting chance." Ryan said as he headed for the confession box and held open the door.

"You have to come with us Ryan. They will kill you." Kyrie pleaded while carrying Anthony's body over.

"Ryan, you can't." Rose implored through a flood of tears.

"I must, we won't all survive this."

"Let me stay." Kyrie offered trying to hand Anthony's limp body over. He was unconscious now.

"I can't carry him, it has to be me who stays." Ryan added.

"I'm not leaving without you." Rose insisted trying to force Ryan through the door.

"It's too late. I've already took the poison..." Ryan finalised.

The room fell deafly silent, except the sound of digging below.

"...That's what that pill was. I'm not being turned into one of them. I won't become a weapon for them to use."

Kyrie and Rose didn't know what to say or do.

"Now go!" Ryan demanded.

It was a whole ten minutes later when the first werewolf finally burst through the floorboards. Ryan was ready with his gun aimed. He fired one single shot. The werewolf fell back down the hole with a lame thud. Another one squeezed through the floor in its place. Ryan put him down too, then a third. The fourth werewolf took the last of his bullets to put down so he was forced to use a piece of floorboard to dispatch a fifth. He managed a sixth using his bare hands. The seventh knocked him down before biting into his neck. As he bled profusely from the wound in his neck he gargled a lame laugh through the blood that was filling up his windpipe. The werewolf suddenly howled in discomfort, it had been poisoned. It wallowed in pain before falling to the floor in a lump, dead. As more werewolves filled the room Ryan Neil died with a smile on his face, surrounded by the seven werewolves he had managed to take with him.

When the girls entered the confession box they found themselves in a tunnel. They followed it for what seemed like miles before they arrived at what had been cleverly disguised as a drainage tunnel. They key for the padlock was in a box nearby the exit. As they entered the darkness outside they both ran as fast as they could for as long as they could. As the werewolf howls began to gain on them they found themselves at the foot of a hill, with Penshaw monument proudly looking down on them.

CHAPTER 64

BACK DOOR TO HELL

Helena was disappointed when all of her sisters started getting up. She loved them and was keen to get on with the spell, but she wanted to stay in the moment with Rachel for just a little longer. It had been a funny few months for Helena, ever since Elathan suddenly appeared in her sitting room to tell her that her husband was having an affair. But at the same time, she wouldn't change it for the world. She had moved on from her cheating husband and met a new partner, a better partner. One she was excited about a future with. She had found all five of her sisters, sisters that she never knew she even had, and she was about meet her mother. A mother that she never got to know because she died when Helena was just a baby.

It was tense and nobody spoke as they all began to gather in the middle of the factory around the cauldron. Everything and everyone was in place. Their favourite possessions and the ingredients they needed for the spell had been soaking in the green bubbling fluid overnight. The muffled yelling of the six souls still locked in the sacrifice chamber just behind them. All they had to do now was begin the chant. Eager to get on with the spell Holly approached the cauldron and put out her hands.

"Everyone ready?" Holly asked.

Nobody answered, but one by one the sisters copied Holly and joined hands until they formed a perfect circle around the cauldron, Rachel was stationed above and had one eye on the CCTV footage outside and one eye on what was happening below. The smell of freshly mown grass, vinegar and burning plastic filled the room.

"Let's do this." Holly said with a deep breath.

Rachel glanced down lovingly at Helena who noticed and gave her a little wink.

"Let us now chant." Holly interrupted loudly. Her tone was serious.

"Terra mortuis debemus offerre panem. Sex pro animae nostrae." They all tried to chant together, the words were second nature now, but their timings were way off from one another.

Alyson was not surprised that nothing had happened. She tried her best not to laugh at their foul attempt.

"Follow my lead." Holly demanded before restarting.

"Terra mortuis debemus offerre panem. Sex pro animae nostrae." They all said in relative unison.

A green flame rose from the cauldron, turned blue and danced around as if it was alive, before settling back down into the green bubbling fluid. It gave them hope. They all tried again.

"Terra mortuis debemus offerre panem. Sex pro animae nostrae." They shouted in unison.

Their vim and vigour prevailed as the flame jumped out of the cauldron and headed straight for the sacrifice chamber. Their cries were evident as the blue flame entered the chamber stealing their very souls away. All of the girls winced and held onto one another trying their best to ignore the screams of the sacrificed. Rachel watched in awe as the exuberant flame returned to the cauldron and danced around its rim. Suddenly the flame disappeared and became a beam of red light which swelled from cauldron to roof. It was a portal. Lightning triggered around its funnelled edges with crashes of thunder. A huge white flash appeared and moved to one of the six red circles the girls had spray-painted onto the factory floor. It was a man dressed in a peculiar-looking white robe with strange red symbols painted on it, he looked more relieved than surprised to be there.

Rachel was so transfixed with the spell she did not notice the two vehicles quickly approaching the building on the CCTV monitor. A jeep ahead of another car. Another flash of white light and another soul escaped the portal landing in another red circle. It was Elathan wearing his usual attire. The sisters were so pleased to see him that they almost let go of one another and ruined the spell.

They girls waited impatiently for another white flash, this time it was what looked like a man, only his entire muscular body was blue. He tried to immediately leave his circle but was clearly pinned to the floor; he looked around the room as another flash lit up the warehouse. This time it was the daemon Eblis, dressed in his purple suit. Helena was pleased to see and hear that he wasn't chewing on anything. He had a smug smile upon his face.

The girls looked towards the two remaining circles painted on the floor eager to see their mother Emily land in one of them. But their attention was taken away as a Jeep suddenly crashed through the side of the factory and into the office area just ahead of them. Melissa looked angrily up at Rachel who had not done her job.

"Do not break the circle." Holly demanded as another flash of white light occurred. This time it was what looked like a pair of trainers, tracksuit bottoms and a hoodie with nobody inside. It was like a ghost, more shadow than physical being. Rachel angrily picked up the gun from the table and began firing down at the figures that entered the building through the hole the Jeep had caused. Chora, Paige and Doc were forced to dive for cover behind a few of the many metal columns that stood in the factory while Winwood, who was in the driver's seat of the Jeep, only just managed to get out of the vehicle as it burst into flames.

As another flash of white light filled up the final red circle the girls were relieved to see it was their mother. As quick as it began the lighting dissipated, the thunder quietened and the portal of light disappeared back into the cauldron. The green bubbling fluid fizzled away until the cauldron was empty. The spell was complete.

CHAPTER 65

HELL ON EARTH

David, Trigger and Legitus all got out of the car and marched towards the newly created hole in the side of the factory. Trigger handed over two lightning pistols, one to David, one to Legitus, before pulling his own from the back of his jeans. As they neared the factory David suddenly froze. He could hear the gunfire, the spells that were being cast, the shouting inside, and it was all too much for him. He was too scared to go ahead, too scared to run away. It wasn't the first time he had felt like this, but it was the first time in a while. He thought (or rather hoped) he was over this crippling fear.

"David. What's up, come on." Legitus shouted back to him.

But David was stuck, rooted to the spot with a disappointed look on his face. He was trying his best not to imagine all the bad things that could have already happened. All the bad things that could be about to happen. He was terrified. David could do nothing but watch as Trigger whispered something to Legitus who nodded and ran into the factory. Trigger then came back for David.

"I know it's really scary. But I promise you, you will be okay." Trigger tried.

David wanted to help, more than anything, but he was too scared to. He didn't want to die. He didn't want his friends to die.

"Look, you can do whatever you want to do mate, and you'll still be one of us whatever happens. But I have to go in there because our friends need us. They need you, especially your girlfriend." Trigger said before patting David on the back and running into the factory.

The sound of the bullets echoed through the factory as Rachel finished her third and final clip of ammo, she still hadn't hit anything. Trigger and Legitus ran in to support Paige and Doc who were pinned in the middle of the factory, ducking out of the way of fire-balls and ice-spikes to return fire at the huge group that had just completed the spell. Winwood and Chora were also firing from the burning office. So far, they had managed to electrocute two of the targets who lay unconscious on the floor ahead of them. One was a man dressed in a white robe with weird symbols on it, the other was a man with blue skin.

*****

Outside David was still trying his best to push himself to go into the factory.

"Come on David, they need you. Chora needs you." He said aloud to himself. With a deep breath, he forced his left foot forward along the floor, and then his right. Then he took a small but meaningful footstep, and then another, and then another. Slowly but surely, he was edging himself towards the factory.

As the girls found safety behind the sacrifice chamber they took turns hugging their mother Emily, who looked younger than they did. She was so pleased to see them that she was crying.

"Who are these people?" Elathan said interrupting the mini-reunion.

"No idea." Holly replied before firing a fire-bolt around the corner to show her mother what she was capable of.

Unbeknown to her, it hit Doc square in the chest knocking him to the floor. Paige ran over to him rubbing his chest to put out the impending fire. It burnt her hands and his chest, but nothing too serious. She pulled him back into cover as he caught his breath. Winwood started firing his lightning gun at the ceiling above the crowd, trying to draw them out from hiding.

"We are sitting ducks here. What should we do?" Helena asked while firing the falling tiles away from the group and shattering them into a nearby wall.

"Have you ever been to Kielder Forest?" Emily asked.

"No why?" Melissa asked confused about why that was important right now.

"Cos that's where we are going. Elathan, Eblis start skipping everyone out of here." Emily demanded before flailing her hands around creating a ten-foot-high tornado which she let go into the room. It whistled around the factory making those in cover run for cover elsewhere.

David walked into the factory with his head and his gun held high. His hands were shaking but that didn't sully the determined look on his face. He supported Paige and Trigger who were now concentrating their fire on Rachel, who had since ditched the gun for magick.

"So glad you could make it." Trigger shouted over the noise of ice spells crashing around them. David couldn't help but smile, he was so proud of himself.

Meanwhile, at the other end of the room. Winwood was surprised to see that two suited men had suddenly appeared next to the two unconscious bodies on the floor. Before he could figure out what was happening all four of them disappeared into thin air.

"Daemons." Winwood grunted before getting out from cover and firing a burst of shots towards the sacrifice chamber, Chora, Doc and Legitus followed suit. As Margaret tried to glimpse the battlefield she got hit in the chest by a lightning bullet from Chora's gun. The electrocution pulsed right through her body and she staggered around before falling backwards against the factory wall, knocking herself out. Margaret limp body was skipped away by Elathan, while Eblis took the Elemental (The being that looked more like a shadow than a person).

Emily created a shield of energy and walked out from cover. The lightning bullets fizzled out against the invisible ball that surrounded her. Winwood decided to get to cover but found his feet were stuck to the ground. He looked down to see a wall of ice moving up from his feet. Before he could plead for help he found himself frozen solid. As Chora noticed she dropped her gun and ran straight towards him punching the ice block around him to try and break him free.

Emily was next to disappear from the room along with Alyson. Only four witches now remained, Holly, Helena, Melissa and Rachel and they were no match for the hail of bullets being fired in their direction. Rachel grew impatient as she hid from the hail of lighting bullets being fired around her. She decided to make a run for it and filled the air with black smoke in which to make her get away.

Paige, Trigger and David fired a bunch of shots through the black fog. She managed to deflect one as she ran along the upper level towards the stairs. But as she ran a second bullet sizzled into her back and she winced with pain. Unable to control her body she lost her balance and fell forwards over the edge of the balcony of the upper level. Nobody saw her fall to the floor, but everyone heard it. She hit the floor with a horrible thud and blood began cascading from her head like a waterfall.

As Elathan and Eblis skipped Holly and Melissa from the room, Helena looked over to the stairs desperate to see her girlfriend. As the smoke began to fade she spotted her body on the floor in a pool of blood. The shock on Trigger's face didn't stop him being her target. She walked across the room deflecting the bullets fired at her with ease. Trigger felt the murderous cold of stone nipping at his skin as Helena froze him like a statue. It took three lightning bullets before she fell to her knees. But it wasn't enough, she still had the strength to levitate Trigger's stone body into the ceiling splintering him into a thousand fragmented pebbles. Elathan and Eblis returned for Helena and her girlfriends cadaver before they disappeared from the factory for the final time. With nobody left to fight the vampires just stood there subdued by shock, crippled in sorrow.

CHAPTER 66

AFTERMATH

Helena found herself surrounded by woodland. She swung around and grabbed Elathan by the collar.

"Take me back." She demanded with a furious rage.

The birds and wildlife squawked and scurried away. Elathan did not respond. He simply put his head down and ignored her demands.

"Take me back. Now!" She shouted in desperation.

He again remained muted.

"Let me kill them or I will kill you." Helena offered with a tighter grip of his collar.

"Helena!" A voice shouted distracting her. Helena turned to see her mother down on the floor holding Margaret's limp body. Helena ran over shocked.

"What happened?" Helena said holding Margaret's hand while her mother held her neck checking her pulse.

"She took one of them bullets, fell back and hit her head." Emily informed.

"I took three and I'm…" Helena started, but didn't finish.

*****

The vampires hurried back to the Libra base squashed into a single car like sardines. It was a wonder they weren't stopped by the police either as they sped through the traffic back to the base. Winwood was free from the block of ice, but he was freezing cold and unconscious. As soon as they got back Paige and Doc rushed him straight into the Med bay and hooked him up to all sorts of machinery.

"What happened to him?" Celeste worried.

"Freezing spell." Chora informed.

"Where's Trigger?" Torus asked as he noticed the missing man.

Nobody could bring themselves to tell him, but their reaction told him and Celeste everything. Torus fell to his knees as it dawned on him. Everybody else followed him in grief. As quickly as their sorrow began, it ended with the base alarm ringing in their ears. Everybody ran to the defence room without a word. As Chora looked through some of the vitals on the monitor she was relieved to learn it wasn't the witches. This was something else.

The scanner picked up a human, a werewolf and something unidentified. Torus quickly grabbed Paige's gun and joined Chora, David and Legitus in the lift which shot-up to the surface. As the lift climbed up David couldn't help but realise the similarities with when he first arrived at the Libra base, only this time he was on the other side.

"Set the guns to kill mode." Chora informed as they reached the surface and began scanning the area.

"Are you sure?" Legitus asked.

Now that Winwood was incapacitated, Chora was in charge and she was ruthless in her determination.

"Don't forget that Trinity base was attacked recently, nineteen dead and we have the Crown Prince to protect. Just don't shoot unless attacked first." Chora confirmed.

It was night and it was increasingly difficult to see anything at all. The only movement around them was the forest's wildlife that was scurrying away. Kyrie found them before they found the strangers. She stopped still in her tracks as she found herself face to face with four people and four guns. She carefully placed Anthony on the floor and put her hands in the air as Rose caught up with her and immediately did the same.

"What are you doing here?" Chora demanded finger on trigger.

"Ryan sent us. He said you would help. There's a pack of werewolves behind us." Rose pleaded.

"Where is he?" Torus asked.

There was a delay as none of them knew how to answer.

"Where is he?" Chora reiterated.

"He didn't make it... he sacrificed himself so we could get here." Kyrie regretfully informed.

"Where's Anthony?" David questioned as he realised who he was face to face with. The bigger of the two women pointed down to the body that was lying on the floor. David ran over to check despite Chora's yell of "Wait." David recognised Anthony despite the lack of light that was offered to him, but he didn't look well.

"What's wrong with him." David asked feeling his cold demeanour.

"He's been bitten by a werewolf." Kyrie briefed, her hands still pinned in the air.

"We have to help him." David implored through a rising panic. He'd already lost two good friends tonight, he wasn't about to lose another.

"Torus help him get the body down to the med bay." Chora ordered, her suspicious eyes not leaving Rose and Kyrie.

The pair carried the body off towards the lift and headed down into the base. Chora and Legitus still had their guns pointed.

"Please we don't have long." Rose begged with a glance behind. She could sense the chasing packs' imminent arrival.

"Where's the werewolf." Chora asked.

"The pack will be here any second." Kyrie pleaded.

"Where. is. the werewolf." Chora repeated louder.

"Let us in and we will talk about it." Rose tried.

There was a pause. Kyrie realised she didn't have a choice, but she could still give Rose a chance. She swallowed her own fear and spoke.

"It's me. I'm the werewolf." Kyrie admitted.

Chora flicked a smile then fired her gun. It hit the werewolf square in the chest. Kyrie was pleased to turn around and see it was one of the scouts who were following them.

"Quickly. Follow us." Chora motioned to the pair who immediately did as they were told.

As Chora, Legitus, Rose and Kyrie descended down into the base, the woodland above them filled with werewolves. Legitus and Chora marched the pair straight to one of the bedrooms and locked them in one together.

"I'm sorry. It's necessary for the time being." She apologised before disappearing.

Rose and Kyrie didn't argue. Anthony was being looked after and they were safe for now, that was all that mattered.

Chora and Legitus ran back up to the control room. Chora sat in the chair and pressed a button. A turret fired a couple of warning shots into the air. An action that the werewolves ignored as they continued sniffing the trail that they were following. Chora fired another warning shot that was again ignored.

"Very well. Let's go hot." Chora reasoned before pressing a big red button. Hidden turrets folded out from trees and rose up from the floor unleashing short bursts of gunfire at the werewolves. A couple were injured, a couple were neutralized, the rest dispersed and ran away with their tails between their legs. The wolves stopped on the edge of the woodland where Kayzor was stood waiting for them in his bulky human form.

"Do not worry pack. We will be back to avenge them." Kayzor barked before turning back into a wolf and trotting off into the night.

TO BE CONTINUED...

David Sixsmith, Anthony Starkey, Helena Pearce and company will return in...

VOLUME VI: DAYBREAK

The next book in the "Apocalypse Genesis" series will be.

VOLUME II: GUARDIANS OF THE ATMOS

*****

For more information about myself, or the Apocalypse Genesis series, please follow me on twitter.

@JamieRichmond16

*****

Special Thanks

Firstly, let me thank Holmeside Writers (my local writing group) and its members for encouraging me, supporting me and giving me the confidence to put my work out there. Extra thanks to author Alan Parkinson for answering hundreds of my questions.

Secondly, let me thank Bryony Anne Ryan for designing my wonderful cover art. She has literally brought my ideas to life. To see some more of her fantastic work please check out her website.

www.bryonyaryan.portfoliobox.net

Last but not least, my thanks go to Clare H, who is helping me build a website to showcase all of my work.

Printed in Great Britain
by Amazon